Dora Russell

Crsus's Widow

A Novel. Vol. 1

Dora Russell

Crsus's Widow
A Novel. Vol. 1

ISBN/EAN: 9783337045678

Printed in Europe, USA, Canada, Australia, Japan

Cover: Foto ©Andreas Hilbeck / pixelio.de

More available books at **www.hansebooks.com**

CRŒSUS'S WIDOW

A Novel

BY

DORA RUSSELL

AUTHOR OF "FOOTPRINTS IN THE SNOW," "THE VICAR'S GOVERNESS,"

"ANNABEL'S RIVAL," "BENEATH THE WAVE," "QUITE TRUE,"

"THE MINER'S OATH," ETC., ETC.

IN THREE VOLUMES

VOL. I.

LONDON

JOHN AND ROBERT MAXWELL

MILTON HOUSE, SHOE LANE

FLEET STREET

MDCCCLXXXIII

CONTENTS.

TILLOTSON & SON, BOLTON.

CRŒSUS'S WIDOW.

CHAPTER I.

THE PAST AND PRESENT.

HE lived in a great house, the rich man
whom his friends and neighbours jestingly
called Crœsus. He was very rich, as this
jest-name implied, for he had money and
houses and land, and there was nothing in
all the world that could be *bought* which was
not his.

But there are some things that no wealth
can buy—can a man " add one cubit unto his
stature "; or stop the stealthy footprints of
approaching age? Neither could Mr. John
Trelawn buy—what perhaps he prized the

most on earth—the love of the woman to
whom he had been married for five long years.

She was sitting waiting for him, this woman,
on the evening when this story of her life
begins. She was young still; young, fragile,
and dark-eyed; and she sighed wearily as she
sat alone waiting for her husband, for her
thoughts had wandered far away from the
present to the past.

Let us for a moment look with her down
that long vista. We shall see a girl then; a
girl in her fresh bright youth, though youth
and hope were about all the good gifts that
fortune had given her. She was the daughter
of a man who had failed in business, and had
started afresh with diminished capital and
credit. Anxious days and anxious nights had
succeeded. With a sickly wife, two handsome
girls, and a boy to provide for, carking care
had followed and pursued Mr. Henry Sudely,
of Warbrooke, like a shadow. But he had one
true friend; a friend bound to him alike by
bonds of near relationship and love. This was
his only sister—a sister many years his senior
who had done well in life, and had (in her day)
made the most of her charms, and was now

Lady Stainbrooke, the wife of General Sir Thomas Stainbrooke, K.C.B.

Thus, when Lady Stainbrooke returned from India, after spending the best part of twenty years there, she was able materially to help her oppressed brother, Mr. Henry Sudely.

She went down to her native town, Warbrooke, to stay with her relations, but she did not enjoy her visit. She had left her brother a stout, jovial-looking, prosperous man, and on her return she found him bent, white-haired, and careworn.

"Can it possibly be you, Henry?" she said, gazing at Mr. Sudely's worn face in astonishment; and "Henry" was also looking at her the same moment in sad surprise.

Twenty years had made a great change. She was an old woman now; old, brown, and withered, with a front of false hair placed low on her wrinkled forehead, and she also dressed very eccentrically, bringing out "gowns" (as she called them) which she must have had for thirty years. But she was kind, and had a sense of humour and a sharp tongue of her own, of which she made abundant use.

She felt very sorry for her brother. He had

been almost a boy in her mind all through the years of her absence, and to see him so care-worn and changed touched her worldly and hardened heart.

"I will take your two girls by turns and get them off, Henry," she told Mr. Sudely. "Sir Thomas will not object, as they are both pre-sentable, and, poor man, he likes to be seen with pretty girls still!" And Lady Stainbrooke laughed.

Thus it was arranged that Nora Sudely left her father's house and went to live with her aunt, Lady Stainbrooke. She had never seen her uncle-by-law, Sir Thomas Stainbrooke, and felt rather nervous when the cab in which her aunt and she were driving stopped before the house, in town, which Sir Thomas and Lady Stainbrooke had taken for the season.

"Now, my dear," said Lady Stainbrooke, as they approached Warwick Square, where this house was situated, "I am going to give you a little advice. I wish Sir Thomas to like you, and therefore you must flatter him and make yourself pleasant to him, for however old a man is he is always open to flattery."

Nora Sudely laughed—a girl's fresh, glad laugh.

"Very well, aunt," she said; "and do you flatter him too?"

"I'm married to him, my dear, so I've no occasion to do so," replied the old lady, drily.

But when a few minutes later Nora was introduced to the General, who was a little, shuffling, rheumatic old man, she thought it would be almost impossible to flatter him.

"This is Nora Sudely," screamed Lady Stainbrooke at the utmost extent of her voice, so as to reach her husband's deaf ears.

The General bowed, and then smiled blandly, and showed both rows of his yellow, false teeth.

"Hope you're well?" he said. "Glad to see you—always glad to see a pretty face, ha, ha, ha!" And Sir Thomas laughed a peculiar, cackling, hollow laugh, which somehow or other set your teeth on edge.

Nora Sudely laughed too, and looked with astonishment at the first General she had ever seen.

"Hope your father and mother are well?" continued Sir Thomas.

"They are both very well, I think," said Nora, raising her voice to its highest pitch.

"What do you say?" asked Sir Thomas,

coming nearer to Nora. "I don't exactly catch
what you say—I've a cold, and that makes me
a little deaf, I think."

"You have always a cold, then," screamed
Lady Stainbrooke.

"What are you screaming about, madam?"
said the little General, sharply. "Ladies
should never scream—they look ugly, horribly
ugly, when they scream."

"They shouldn't have deaf husbands, then,"
retorted Lady Stainbrooke.

"I'm not deaf generally, madam," answered
the General. "I've a cold; I suppose you
sometimes have a cold?"

"Very often," replied Lady Stainbrooke,
grimly. "But I want you to hear this even
in spite of your cold, as you call it. Nora
Sudely, as you know, has come to stay
with us, and you must try to make her visit
agreeable."

"Charmed to do so, I am sure," said the
General, once more looking approvingly at
Nora. "Any man would be charmed to have
such a pretty young lady to stay in his house."
And the General once more emitted the hollow,
cackling sound which he called a laugh.

"Thank you for the compliment, Sir Thomas," said Nora Sudely.

"No compliment," said the old soldier. "It's truth—I like pretty women; always liked 'em." And he gave his frightful cackle again.

"We must take her about a little; we must take her to the opera," said Lady Stainbrooke.

"Certainly," said the General; "any time—sooner the better."

"There, my dear," said Lady Stainbrooke, turning to Nora; "you see what it is to have a good-looking face! If I had told Sir Thomas that any angular, copper-tinted relation of mine was coming to stay with us, he probably would have sworn at me; but he's quite delighted to have you."

"What are you mumbling about, madam?" said Sir Thomas, looking at his wife, for he hated not to hear what was going on. "You are one of those women who are always mumbling or screaming. Now, if you spoke in a steady, even-toned voice, even with my bad cold I could hear you."

"Very well, I'll try," said Lady Stainbrooke, who was anxious for her niece's sake not to quarrel with her irate little spouse.

"I should be pleased to ride with you, Miss Sudely," said the General the next minute, gallantly, "but the confounded climate of India still affects me, and I'm a little stiff in the joints."

"You are too old to think of riding," shouted Lady Stainbrooke.

"Nothing of the kind! Speak for yourself, madam. Many men, a great many years my senior, ride, but we old soldiers, Miss Sudely—we get battered with hard service before our time."

"Yes," said Nora, very loudly; "but it's a noble profession."

"I think so," said the General. "It's a gentleman's profession—not a vulgar, money-making, pettifogging business such as some men, born of good families, now follow. Yes, Miss Sudely, I'm glad you like soldiers."

Poor old man! He was aches and pains all over, yet he had his vanity still, and liked (as his wife had told her niece) to be flattered and made much of.

With this quaint old couple, then, Nora Sudely found herself domiciled a few days before she had reached her nineteenth birthday.

She did not find it very lively. Lady Stainbrooke had only a very small circle of acquaintance, for all the General's family and almost all his old friends had passed away during his lengthened sojourn in India. But some old Indians like himself came occasionally to dine at the dull house in Warwick Square. Then Nora would sit and listen to dingy tales, the actors of which had mostly disappeared; she would hear gossip that had tickled ears which now were deaf, and stories of the mischief wrought by bright eyes now dulled or closed. It was a strange life for a young girl, and while Lady Stainbrooke and her friends were chuckling over lost reputations, Nora Sudely was dreaming her first bright dream of love.

She had not left her father's house heart-whole. About six months before Lady Stainbrooke's arival in England Nora had made the acquaintance of a young painter who had gone to Warbrooke (the town where the Sudely's lived) for his summer holiday, and for the purpose of sketching some of the neighbouring scenery.

Nora Trelawn, now sitting in her husband's grand house, waiting for his return, saw in the

past at that moment a picture which love had
painted on her heart.

A girl, bright, sparkling, and happy; and a
man, earnest, impassioned, with a profile like
a Greek model, standing before her, in a soft
evening in June. He was holding her hand,
and words, if not of love, at least of tenderness,
were on his lips.

The girl turned aside, half coquettishly.

"Ah," she said, "I daresay you have often
made these pretty speeches before?"

"Never," answered the painter; "my loves
have all hitherto been ideal ones."

"Very different to the real one," laughed
the girl.

"Yes, very different," he replied, candidly.
"Your face is not quite perfect, you know,
Nora, and you are a brown little girl instead
of a pink and white goddess; but to me you
are—"

"Well, what, sir?"

"Beautiful," said the painter: "for I see
your sweet soul in your face."

.   .   .   .   .   .

A brief love scene—a rift of light still shining
through the dull, grey, monotonous colouring

which now for five long years had surrounded rich John Trelawn's young wife. And how did these love passages with the handsome painter end?

They ended thus. Nora Sudely went, as we have seen, to live with her aunt, Lady Stainbrooke, and Lady Stainbrooke meant conscientiously to keep her word to her brother, and get his penniless girl married as best she could. But one day, at the opening of the Academy, Nora stood so long before a picture in which her aunt saw nothing particular to admire, that Lady Stainbrooke put on her gold-rimmed glasses and glanced at the number and the artist's name in her catalogue.

"Humph!" said Lady Stainbrooke, "W. D. Vyner. Well, I don't think much of him, at any rate!"

"He is a friend of mine, and a very clever artist," said Nora Sudely. And her face flushed.

"He may be a great friend of yours, my dear, but he's not a great painter, I can tell him, with my compliments," answered Lady Stainbrooke.

As these words passed her lips both Lady Stainbrooke and Nora heard a light short laugh

from someone in the crowd behind them. Nora
turned round, and her face flushed more deeply
still as she did so.

"Mr. Vyner! You here!" she said, and she
held out a little trembling hand.

"Yes," he answered. "So you and this lady
were criticising my daub?"

It was the handsome artist who had stood
hand-in-hand with Nora on that bright evening
in June, which she remembered only too well.
He had left Warbrooke, promising to return,
but before he had done so Nora had quitted
her father's house; nevertheless the memory
of Mr. Vyner had not faded from her mind.

And now, as the two stood exchanging
greetings amid the London crowd, the girl's
dark eyes shining and smiling in the artist's
face, Lady Stainbrooke, glancing from one to
the other, at once guessed their secret.

"My aunt, Lady Stainbrooke," said Nora,
timidly. "Mr. Vyner."

"So you think I shall never be a great painter,
Lady Stainbrooke?" said Vyner, smilingly
looking at the old lady after his introduction.

Lady Stainbrooke felt a little disconcerted.
Mr. Vyner was such a good-looking man that it

seemed impossible to a woman to say anything rude to him. She therefore did not hesitate to make a little invention.

"You mistook my observation, Mr. Vyner," she said, graciously. "It was the painter of this picture" (and she pointed with her glasses at a picture hanging near Vyner's) "that I said would never be great."

"Yet he is great," answered Vyner, somewhat grimly. "But," he added, "will you come and look at another picture of mine? I don't think much of this one myself."

The two ladies followed Vyner's tall, slight form until he stopped before a very striking picture. Here was a wild sea coast, and two brown, stalwart, excited fishermen hauling in a capsized boat.

"These rough subjects suit me best," said Vyner, folding his arms, and standing looking fixedly at his work.

Lady Stainbrooke put up her glasses, and also examined the picture.

"This is good," she said, at length; "very good."

The painter smiled. Praise was sweet to him, as it is to us all; but it was sweeter still because it fell on Nora Sudely's ears.

Then Lady Stainbrooke looked at the painter
himself, examining him critically through her
gold-rimmed glasses, as she had examined his
picture.

"I took my niece to the National Gallery
the other day, Mr. Vyner," she said. "I'm
an old-fashioned woman, and I like the old
painters."

Vyner was now in his element. His large,
handsome grey eyes lit with enthusiasm when
he spoke of the old masters and their great
works, and Lady Stainbrooke listened well
pleased to his energetic words.

"We are pigmies," he said, "we modern
men beside these giants. Ah! Lady Stainbrooke," and he stretched out one of his white,
nervous hands, "if I could but pourtray my
dreams."

Lady Stainbrooke nodded her head.

"That is ever the cry of genius," she said;
"the imagination outstrips the manual power.
But, young man," she added, "if you have
the divine fire—the gift which no application
or study can give you—you will succeed."

As Lady Stainbrooke spoke, the painter was

standing before her with his head erect, and with his eyes fixed apparently on something far away. Perhaps some ideal picture was passing before him—some grand brain shadow that his hand could never produce. At all events, after standing in this rapt attitude for a few minutes, he gave a restless sigh, and looked once more at Lady Stainbrooke.

"I've been unsettled lately," he said, "unsettled and restless. I have not done my work as I should."

"Perhaps you're in love," said Lady Stainbrooke.

"Perhaps I am," answered Vyner, with an uneasy little laugh; and he glanced at Nora's bright, blushing face as he spoke.

"Well," said Lady Stainbrooke, "as I am not, I would not at all object to some lunch."

The painter escorted the ladies to the refreshment-room, and was very attentive to Lady Stainbrooke. Her ladyship made herself highly agreeable to him, and invited him to call upon her at her house in Warwick Square. Then, as she drove home with Nora after they had parted with Vyner, she heard all about him. He was poor—a struggling man—and no absolute declaration of love had passed between him and Nora.

But the girl felt, as she told her aunt this, that he cared for her. This knowledge, or rather hope, was very sweet to Nora's heart; but it did not at all suit Lady Stainbrooke's views.

The next day Vyner called at Warwick Square, and her ladyship saw him alone. Nora had been sent out on an errand for her aunt, and the painter had received a little note, asking him to visit Lady Stainbrooke at a certain hour.

"I wished to see you, Mr. Vyner," said Lady Stainbrooke, holding out her hand to him with a very good imitation of frankness, "because I hear there has been some romantic nonsense between you and my niece, Nora Sudely."

Vyner's fine skin coloured faintly at this attack.

"I admire Miss Sudely exceedingly," he said.

"Ah yes, my dear sir," said Lady Stainbrooke; "but you cannot live on admiration, nor love either, for that matter. In fact, the

truth is that I have sent for you to appeal to
your honour as a gentleman not to disturb the
girl's peace of mind any further by the sight
of your good-looking face. She is engaged to
be married to my friend Mr. Trelawn, who is a
very worthy and a very rich man, and the less
you see of Nora now the better."

"Engaged!" repeated the painter, and the
colour faded away again from his handsome
face.

"Yes, engaged," repeated Lady Stainbrooke,
quite calmly; "and it is a very good thing, too.
My brother is miserably poor, and his girls are
penniless; and what would become of them if
they did not marry? You see I am quite frank
with you, Mr. Vyner. I like you, and shall be
glad to see you here by-and-bye, and to hear
of your success. But let me get my young
lady married first. Nora herself thinks it is
better not to see you, and I am sure you will
not wish to make her unhappy."

The painter rose to take his leave.

"Certainly not," he said; but even Lady
Stainbrooke's heart misgave her when she saw
the grey, haggard look which stole over the
man's face as he said these words.

As he descended the staircase, another gentleman was ascending it. He knew him by sight. It was John Trelawn, commonly called Crœsus. A stout, big man, with a pale, heavy face, and a very large nose, was John Trelawn. Not one for a young girl to fancy, nor a fitting mate for a bright, sparkling woman like Nora. But he was *rich*. The struggling painter thought this bitterly as he went down stairs. Rich! And what was beauty, genius, tender love even, to *that*?

CHAPTER II.

THE GREAT LEVELLER.

LADY Stainbrooke's little scheme prospered. Nora Sudely was not engaged to Crœsus when Lady Stainbrooke told the painter this piece of news, but Nora Sudely was engaged to Crœsus very soon afterwards.

"My dear," said Lady Stainbrooke to Nora, upon her return from the errand on which her ladyship had sent her to keep her out of the painter's way, "I've had a visit from your friend, Mr. Vyner. Really, he is a very agreeable young man. You remember I asked him if he was in love yesterday at the Academy. Well, I made a very shrewd guess. He has just been telling me all about it. It is some parson's daughter in Suffolk—an absurd affair it seemed at first—no money on either side,

and as I told him, living on love went out with
the Flood!   But the strangest things happen.
This girl has come into a small fortune, and so
the affair is settled."

Nora Sudely listened to these words, and the
bright colour faded out of her cheeks, and the
love-light out of her eyes.   She stood before
her aunt, white and troubled, for a few
moments—a slender girl, trembling, pale, and
heart-stricken—and yet the old woman kept to
her purpose still.

"Aunt," she said at length, trying to speak
calmly, "is this true?

"True, my dear?" repeated Lady Stainbrooke.
"I can, of course, only vouch for its truth as far
as the young man told me, and I can't see any
motive he could have, unless it was true.
By-the-bye, he told me also that he admired
you very much, and altogether made himself
very agreeable."   And Lady Stainbrooke gave
a little laugh.

Nora asked no more questions after this.
She did not speak again of the painter; but Sir
Thomas, a day or two afterwards, said to his
wife—

"That girl is losing her looks—she has lost

her vivacity, her charm—what is the matter with her, madam?"

"She wants change," replied Lady Stainbrooke. "We must take her more about."

So, when Mr. John Trelawn called the same afternoon, to ask his old friend, Lady Stainbrooke, to dine with him at Richmond, her ladyship gladly accepted the invitation.

"The fellow is stupid, and a snob," said Sir Thomas.

"The fellow is rich, and that makes up for everything now-a-days," answered his wife; "and besides, he is an old friend."

This latter recommendation, in one sense of the word, was true. When Lady Stainbrooke had been a handsome young girl in her native town, John Trelawn's father had lived and made a great fortune there. Queer stories about the commencement of this fortune were not wanting; but the fact remained that vast ironworks and vast wealth belonged to Mr. John Trelawn, senior, before he retired from all earthly business.

He left one child only — John Trelawn, commonly called Crœsus. This John Trelawn, then had known the handsome Miss Sudely in his awkward boyhood. The handsome Miss Sudely had married an officer and had left Warbrooke while John was at school, but still he had known her. Trouble had come to the Sudely's in the years that had rolled away since then, and greater wealth to the Trelawns. Old Trelawn had been gathered to his fathers, and John Trelawn (Crœsus) was a middle-aged man when Lady Stainbrooke returned to her native town, but still when they met they remembered, or pretended to remember, each other. They remembered each other's names at any rate, and Lady Stainbrooke made herself very agreeable to Crœsus.

Then Crœsus came up to town, and was glad to meet Lady Stainbrooke there. They were in fact mutually useful to each other. John Trelawn knew no one in London; and though Lady Stainbrooke had not a large acquaintance, still she had some friends, and she liked John Trelawn's opera boxes, his dinners at Richmond—in truth, his wealth.

And so she fixed that he was to marry her niece, Nora Sudely, and he did marry her. The girl was not a willing victim, but she yielded to her aunt's representations.

"Think how poor your father is, child; think of what will become of you if you do not marry," urged Lady Stainbrooke ; and so, sad, silent, almost broken-hearted, Nora Sudely accepted her fate.

She married John Trelawn because she believed that the man she loved was about to be, or was, married to another woman. She married John Trelawn because he was rich, and because she could help her father and her ailing mother, and her young brother and sister. But she never was the same woman again.

John Trelawn bought a grand new house in South Kensington ; he bought a villa by the river ; and sometimes he took his young wife down to the big house at Warbrooke, where his father had died, and they entertained Nora's family and his old friends there ; but everything always seemed very dull to Nora.

She tried to do her duty, and indeed did it, as well as she was able, but she was not happy. A nameless dreariness and dulness always possessed her. Her sister married well, her young brother entered the army, her mother died in comfort, and years passed away, but no children came to her, and there was no brightness in her life Nora told herself, and she often wondered why people cared to live, and why they fretted and fumed about things that seemed of so little worth.

At last one day (on her birthday) John Trelawn presented his young wife with a set of such rich and costly diamonds that it was scarcely possible for any woman to see them and know that they were hers without delight.

So at least said Lady Stainbrooke, who had helped to choose them, and it must be admitted that Nora felt a slight glow of gratitude and affection for " John," as she gazed upon his magnificent gift.

He gave them to her in the grand house at South Kensington. Sir Thomas and Lady Stainbrooke dined with them on the same day, and after dinner her ladyship (having partaken very freely of "John's" champagne) said to Nora—

" Ah, my dear, you may thank me now, I think, that by a little innocent artifice I parted you from a beggarly painter."

Nora's face flushed, and she put her hand quickly to her side. Then she asked, almost calmly—

"What artifice did you use, aunt?"

"I invented a young woman, that was all," replied Lady Stainbrooke, with a little laugh.

"Then Mr. Vyner never told you that he was engaged—never told you anything at all, I suppose?" said Nora, still calmly.

Lady Stainbrooke nodded her head.

"He told me he admired you, and I told him—had the sense and discretion to tell him— that *you* were engaged, Nora, and you see how well it has all turned out. You have every- thing—diamonds—in fact, everything a woman can desire."

"Except happiness," said Nora, in a low tone, and she left her aunt—left her diamonds lying in their grand new velvet cases; and the old woman, as she looked at them with her blinking eyes, acknowledged to herself that John Tre- lawn's champagne had been too much for her, and had stolen away her wit.

"I should never have told her," she thought ; but Nora said nothing more to her aunt about Mr. Vyner.

Yet a few months later (for the first time since her marriage), she met him. Nora was at the Academy with some friends, and in the

crowd, just as she had seen him long ago—her
eyes fell upon his never-to-be-forgotten face.

She held out her hand to him, and for a
moment or two no word was exchanged between them. Then he said :

"It is a long time since we met—Mrs.
Trelawn.

"Yes," answered Nora, "a long time indeed—
and," she added quickly, her pale face flushing,
"you—you are not married, then ?"

"No," answered Vyner, and his face, too,
flushed.

"My aunt—Lady Stainbrooke—told me long
ago—before my own marriage — before my
engagement, in fact—that you were about to
be married," hesitated John Trelawn's wife,
with trembling lips and moistening eyes ;
"otherwise, Mr. Vyner—"

She said nothing more, and for a minute
Walter Vyner made no reply. He stood
there, looking at the once bright face
which years ago had been his sweetest ideal
of womanhood. It was a bright face no
longer. Nora Trelawn was scarcely pretty
now, with large, sad, dark eyes, and a
weary look somehow all over the small,

regular features, that the painter remembered
so attractive and charming.

"So!" he said presently, still looking at
Nora, "that old woman spoilt two lives, then?"

"She spoilt mine," said Nora, in a low tone;
"but—we must not speak of it now."

All around them was the crowd. Other
tragedies and comedies were perhaps being
played on the same stage, but Walter Vyner
and Nora Trelawn thought not of these. They
only remembered when they had stood hand-
in-hand, that summer evening long ago, and
dreamed of a future that was not to be. It
was but a common story, but as the painter
kept watching Nora's face, he knew he had
been regretted with no common regret, and
loved with an abiding love that had not passed
away.

.   .   .   .   .   .

They never met again for years. W. D. Vyner
rose in fame after this, and John Trelawn
(Crœsus) bought one or two of his pictures and
hung them up in his big houses, but never
noted how often his young wife's dark eyes
would wander to the canvas on the walls
which Walter Vyner's hand had made to live.

And so years passed on. Crœsus grew richer and stouter, but there was no other change. They had been married five years on the evening when Nora was sitting waiting for her husband—waiting for him, but not thinking of him—thinking of the past which Lady Stainbrooke's little artifice had spoilt.

Presently a heavy footstep was heard on the staircase outside. John Trelawn's wife heard it, and moved slightly, for she knew it was her husband's. A heavy footstep, and a heavy man! A big, dull man was John Trelawn, though no fool, and kindly-hearted withal, and at times he would indulge in a ponderous sort of jocularity, which his numerous satellites unfailingly pretended to enjoy.

He came into the room now, and laid one of his large hands on his wife's shoulders.

"Well," he said, "and how wags the world with you, my dear?"

Nora smiled faintly.

"Do you expect anyone to dinner, John?" she asked.

"I met Martin and Prosser," answered Crœsus, "and the poor devils looked hungry, and I took compassion. They'll be here directly," continued

Crœsus, looking at his watch, "so I must be off to decorate."

He left the room with a kindly nod to his wife, and by-and-bye Martin and Prosser were ushered in.

Martin and Prosser were little men, just in the same sense that John Trelawn was a great man. Martin and Prosser were poor, and John was rich, and that made the difference between them. They had known John Trelawn all their lives, and they smiled and sighed faintly with envy as they entered the big house and saw on every side the signs of great wealth that it contained.

"How well Crœsus is looking," said Martin, facetiously, to Nora.

"In splendid condition," echoed Prosser.

Nora just answered them, and that was all. She did not care for these early companions of John Trelawn, and one of her objections to the large, dull house at Warbrooke, where they then were, was that such men were never out of it. Still, she could not quarrel with John for being kind to his old friends, but somehow she did not like to live at Warbrooke.

"I will go and see if Mr. Trelawn is ready

for dinner," she said, and so left the room, and Martin and Prosser looked at each other and smiled as she disappeared.

" Uppish ! " said Martin.

" Set a beggar on horseback," suggested Prosser, with a shrug.

Meanwhile Nora had gone up the broad staircase, and was rapping at her husband's dressing-room door.

There was no response. Then she opened the door and went in. John Trelawn was lying on the soft carpet in the middle of the room, with his face downwards. Nora screamed and ran forward. She lifted his head and turned his face round, and when she saw the dull, half-closed eyes and the ghastly colour of his skin, even inexperienced as she was, she knew what had happened.

In a moment—in the midst of his wealth, in the prime of his life—he had been struck down ; the rich man had gone up to dress for dinner, and the grim foe had been waiting for him upstairs. Yes, there was no mistake— Crœsus was dead !

CHAPTER III.

THE WIDOW.

THE sudden death of Crœsus made a great sensation in Warbrooke. A poor man's elegy is soon sung, but our respect at least attends a rich man to his grave.

"Terrible!" said Martin, with a shudder remembering that he also was mortal.

"When he had everything," sighed Prosser, whose pecuniary difficulties had made him find life at times certainly trying.

What Martin and Prosser said was echoed by the whole town. John Trelawn had made few enemies, and even these were awed and silent when they heard the news of the rich man's sudden death.

And the widow? The dark-eyed woman, who had never heard a stern or unkind word

from his lips.   What did she think and say
as she sat in the darkened room, where the
still form lay—the empty shell of the kindly
soul that had given her nothing but love and
costly gifts, ever since she promised to be
his wife,—promised what her heart could not
fulfil ?

It was all over now, and there was bitter
regret in Nora's heart for her own shortcomings.

She sat there remembering how good he had
been, how unfailingly generous and considerate.
He had grudged her nothing, and she had
grudged him even a little love—even a bright
smile or two—for she had been sad, though
uncomplaining, all their wedded days.

But she was not allowed to sit long alone
with her dead.   By the first express after the
news of John Trelawn's sudden death reached
her, Lady Stainbrooke hurried down to Warbrooke to comfort and attend upon her afflicted
niece.   Her ladyship no doubt believed (and
she was a shrewd old woman) that she would
have done the same if Nora had been poor.
But she would not.   In that case she would
have said, " Poor, dear Nora—how sad !"
and sent her a five-pound note.   But in the

case of Crœsus's widow, her sympathy was
active, was gushing.

"Poor child, poor darling!" she said to Sir
Thomas, but Sir Thomas did not respond. Sir
Thomas, indeed, had never taken very kindly
to Crœsus. He came of a different class. His
father had been a distinguished general while
Crœsus's father had been working in a leather
apron at a forge. And the pride of birth clung
to the old soldier. Crœsus might be rich,
"And you women think more of that than
anything else," sneered Sir Thomas Stainbrooke;
but Crœsus was not a gentleman, and this Sir
Thomas could not forgive.

The poor old rheumatic man, close on the
brink of the grave, clung to the badges of his
order still. He, Sir Thomas Stainbrooke, was
not in truth so fine a gentleman as rough John
Trelawn, lying in his darkened room at Warbrooke, once had been. At least he had not
been so honest, so pure of life, so true to his
word, and to the woman he had wed, as
John Trelawn. But these were not Sir Thomas's
ideas about the term of gentleman. He read
that word in a different sense. To him it
meant to be well-born, to be brave, to pay

your debts of honour, and for the rest—. Ah well! Sir Thomas, like many another man who calls himself a gentleman, was not very particular. His mind was prejudiced and very narrow. His love had been gallantry, and his faith—if he had any—was the echo of some parson's words.

But the big ugly man who had died so suddenly at Warbrooke had been larger-minded than this. He had made no professions, but he had given freely and generously of the good gifts which fortune had showered upon him. There were many to regret him as well as his dark-eyed wife. His name had figured largely enough in charity lists, but there were other charities without lists which had benefited still more largely by John Trelawn's honest hand.

So when they carried him to the great family vault, where the first John Trelawn (the founder of their vast fortune) lay in state, there were some true mourners at least who followed the second John Trelawn to his long home. There were other mourners, whose hearts were racked with anxiety beneath the black silken scarves which they wore so decorously. These were the relatives of the dead man—those who

had hopes that they were not quite forgotten
in the will, which it was understood was to
be read after the funeral was over.

But when the will was read, only disappointment awaited them. John Trelawn had left
the whole of his great fortune to his wife, "In
token of the tender love, respect, and affection
which I bear her." In these words he be-
queathed enormous wealth to the woman who
was sitting upstairs, sad and listless. For Nora
had declined to be present when her husband's
will was read. She had not recovered yet from
the shock of his sudden death. His familiar
presence still seemed to haunt her—she could
scarcely realize that she was to hear the loud
voice and the heavy footfall no more.

But the news of her new wealth soon reached
her. Lady Stainbrooke did not wait even for
the lawyer to finish John Trelawn's will, until
she hurried from the room, and went to the
widow.

"My dearest child," she said, embracing
Nora with effusion, "I was determined no one
else should tell you. Your dear husband—
John, my old friend—has acted in the noblest
manner. He has indeed shown how much he

loved you, for he has left you everything."

Nora's pale cheeks slightly flushed, and that was all, when she heard the announcement.

"It is a great position," went on Lady Stainbrooke, with elation. "Nora, you have everything before you now—you can marry—"

"Aunt, aunt, hush!" interrupted Nora, putting up her hand.

"Well, it is a little too soon to speak of it," admitted Lady Stainbrooke, "and naturally you must now feel great respect and affection for the memory of dear John, after hearing the contents of his will. I'm so delighted, my dear child! Nothing is so consoling as money, and it would have been so dreadful if any of these poor relations of his had got anything. There would have been nothing but disputes in that case. Now it is all right, everything is yours; and I hope, my dearest girl, you'll live long to enjoy it." And once more Lady Stainbrooke kissed her widowed niece.

Then Henry Sudely—Nora's father—came into the room. He was a grey-haired man, with the marks of care upon his face, and he also went up and kissed his rich daughter.

"Your aunt has told you, then?" he said.

"Well, my dear, it's a great fortune—may it bring you happiness." And Mr. Sudely sighed.

He was thinking how a little of this wealth —just a very little of it—would have lightened his heavy burdens long ago! Since Nora's marriage he had not wanted money, but he could not forget the sorely-pinched days which preceded it. They had made him old before his time—old, grey-haired, and bowed; and their memory came back to him now in strange contrast with his daughter's enormous wealth.

Nora kissed her father tenderly, and pressed his hand. Then, when Mr. Sudely told her how John Trelawn's will was worded, she became much affected.

"Poor John!" she said. "Poor, poor John!"

She scarcely said anything more than this, but her heart was full of self-reproach and sorrow. How little she had appreciated his great love—how little she had given in return! She kept thinking this while her aunt and her father were talking of John Trelawn's money, and of Nora's future life and position.

"She will make a great match," she heard her aunt say presently, in an undertone; and as

these words fell on her ears, a thought—a
memory—which she instantly tried to banish,
flitted for a moment across Nora's mind.

During the next few days this thought,
this memory, often recurred to her. But she
always checked it. It seemed to her, indeed,
almost a sin to think of any future happiness
which might be in store for her, so soon after
her kindly husband's death.

But as time went on, and weeks passed
away, her life naturally changed. For one
thing, she left the dull house at Warbrooke and
went to the pleasant one in South Kensington,
which John Trelawn had left to her. Her aunt
and Sir Thomas came to stay with her here;
for, as Lady Stainbrooke said, it was not good
for her to be alone, and it was also very con-
venient to her ladyship to live free of expense
with her widowed and wealthy niece.

This arrangement also gave Lady Stainbrooke
a position in society which she had not before
attained. The story of John Trelawn's enormous
wealth had crept into the papers, and when it
became known that all this vast fortune was
left to his dark-eyed young widow, many a
scheming mother sought an opportunity of

making the dark-eyed young widow's acquaintance.

She in fact became known in society as
"Crœsus's Widow." This name was given to
her very shortly after her return to town, and
the house in South Kensington where she lived
soon began to be regarded with great interest.

The first person who called her Crœsus's
Widow was young Lord Seaforth. Lady Seaforth, his widowed mother, was Nora's next-
door neighbour at her house in South Kensington; had been, in fact, her next-door
neighbour for several years when John Trelawn
died.

But Mrs. John Trelawn—however rich—had
been a person of no consequence in Lady
Seaforth's eyes. She would shrug her shoulders
and turn away her head disdainfully when she
saw John's thoroughbreds standing at his door.

"Some rich people I know nothing of," was
her description of the Trelawns, if any of her
set inquired who were the owners of the
thoroughbreds. She, in fact, would have
nothing to say to them; never looked their
way, and utterly ignored that such people as
the Trelawns existed.

But in the five years of Nora's wedded life young Lord Seaforth, the only son of this proud dame, had been running a career which threatened to bring his family's lofty name into the Bankruptcy Court. Nora remembered the young lord, a handsome lad, riding up to his mother's door in his first uniform. He was about four-and-twenty now, and the shadow of his life had fallen on that once bright face.

Lord Seaforth was no longer a handsome lad. He was a young man with a worn, pale face, and wearied-looking eyes, and a bitter tongue. Yet sometimes the sweet boyish smile of old stole round his lips to gladden his mother's anxious heart. For Lady Seaforth loved her son with a tender and devoted love of which she rarely spoke. He was her only child—the one babe born to her before her lord had thrown aside all ties and lived such a life that his wife and he could only part.

The late Lord Seaforth died suddenly abroad, and the young lord, when a boy of seven, inherited estates already hampered and mortgaged to an almost ruinous extent. But during the long minority they had partially recovered, and when Lord Seaforth entered the Guards he had a fair income as well as an old title to begin life with.

Alas, in five years the income was muddled away, and the old name no brighter! A reckless father had been succeeded by a reckless son. There is no good in telling how the money had gone, but it was gone : in diamonds, in expensive pleasures, in a hundred follies. Lord Seaforth at twenty-four was an impoverished, embarrassed man. Some were richer at his expense; but he had lost everything—his belief in human nature, his bright, high spirits, his good looks—all, in fact, that made life worth living for. This was about his state when Nora Trelawn returned to her house in South Kensington a widow; when her proud neighbour, Lady Seaforth, first began to think of her; when young Lord Seaforth first gave her the name of " Crœsus's Widow."

CHAPTER IV.

LADY SEAFORTH.

BETWEEN Nora's drawing-room and Lady Seaforth's there was a well-built, substantial wall. But, one sunny afternoon in April, six months after John Trelawn's death, let us— invisibly—be present at the same moment in the two drawing-rooms.

We must, by all the laws of etiquette, give her ladyship the precedence, and stand for a few moments silent and unobserved in the somewhat old-fashionedly fitted-up room, where a tall, handsome, fair-haired, and still young-looking woman was sitting on a faded yellow satin couch, crying bitterly.

This was Alice Elizabeth, Viscountess Sea- forth; and before her was standing a young man, with a frown upon his brow, and angry words upon his lips. This young man was

Murray, Viscount Seaforth, and the mother was telling the son some bitter truths.

"It has simply come to this," she was saying : "I shall have to break up my establishment, and go abroad to starve ! And when I think how the money has been wasted—what wretches have got it—"

"Abuse does no good, you know, mother," interrupted the young lord.

"No," answered Lady Seaforth, biting her lips ; "but it is hard—very hard—to keep patience with you."

"Perhaps. I admit I'm a good-for-nothing," said Lord Seaforth, and he began walking up and down the long drawing-room.

The mother's eyes followed him. As they did so, a softer look stole into them, for she was recalling his bright boyhood, before the shadow had fallen upon his face. She looked at him for a few moments, and then she rose, dried the tears that still wet her long brown lashes, and, going softly behind her son, she slid her arm through his.

"Murray," she said, "there is only one thing that you can do—you are young, you are good-looking—you must marry for money."

" Precisely," said Murray, turning round and lightly kissing his mother's cheek. " Find me the unfortunate woman, mother, who will have me, and I shall be charmed."

Lady Seaforth did not speak for a moment ; then with a certain hesitation of manner, which showed her own aversion to the scheme that she was about to propose to her son, she said :

"There is a lady next door, Murray—a widow—she is not of our class, for her wealth came to her, I am told, through commerce ; but still she is rich—very rich—and for her position a very ladylike-looking person."

" Her appearance is of no consequence," said Lord Seaforth, shrugging his shoulders.

" Yes, yes, it is," said his mother, with an impatient sigh.

" Not a whit," answered the young lord, scoffingly. " It is her money, not her face, I want ; so it is of no consequence how ugly she is."

" She is not ugly," continued Lady Seaforth. " Nay, she is good-looking. A dark-eyed woman, with rather a sad expression—yes, decidedly good-looking I call her. Her name is Trelawn—Mrs. Trelawn."

"But is she really rich—very rich?" inquired Lord Seaforth.

"Immensely rich, I am told," answered his mother; "something about thirty or forty thousand a year. In fact, Mr. Trelawn always went by the name of Crœsus."

"And Crœsus's widow is next door!" said Lord Seaforth, throwing up his arms with a mock theatrical air. "What a huge piece of luck! When will you introduce me, mother?"

"I have only just made her acquaintance," said Lady Seaforth. "The truth is, it was rather an awkward affair for me to do, as these people have lived next door for four or five years; but of course I never thought of them before."

"Of course! Not, I presume, until the fair lady became Crœsus's widow, and therefore an object of interest to a tender mother with a beggared son."

"You need not sneer, Seaforth. It could not be very agreeable to me, you must know, to make the acquaintance of these people; but for your sake—"

"That is quite understood. But why do you speak of them as *these* people? Surely there are not two rich widows to choose from ?"

"Her aunt, Lady Stainbrooke, is staying
with her. Lady Stainbrooke is the wife of an
old general, and—well, I must confess I think
that *she* is the most objectionable feature of
the whole connection."

At that moment, on the other side of the
wall, in Nora's drawing-room, Lady Stainbrooke was saying—

"My position, my dear, makes me quite her
equal. It is very civil of her to call, certainly ;
but as her son is in the army, and my husband
is an old soldier, there is nothing remarkable
in it."

"I think she has no right to call upon me
as a widow, when she did not call upon me as
a wife," replied Nora, gravely.

"You forget, my dear, that I was not with
you in poor dear John's lifetime," said Lady
Stainbrooke, complacently. "And poor dear
John himself—well, of course, he was very nice
and generous—but still he was not exactly—
how shall I put it ?—not exactly fitted for
Lady Seaforth's society."

"He was good, he was noble," answered
Nora, warmly, and her face flushed, "and that

is better than an old high-sounding title. It
is a *liberty*, I think, of Lady Seaforth to call
upon me now."

"Nonsense, child, nonsense," said Lady
Stainbrooke, good-naturedly. "I had the
highest opinion of poor dear John—did I not
give my dearest child to him, so I must have
had? But there are grades in society that
cannot be forgotten, and that must, and do,
influence everyone. Naturally, now you take
a different position with your large independent
fortune, to what you did when your husband
was alive. You are elegant-looking, you are
young, and you are rich—why, my dear, you
could marry *any one!*"

"But I do not mean to marry any one,"
answered Nora. "Not even a spendthrift
young lord, aunt." And Nora gave a little
laugh.

Nevertheless a day or two after this Nora
accepted Lady Seaforth's invitation to dine
with her alone. Her reason for doing this,
however, was not to meet the spendthrift
young lord. But when Lady Seaforth called
to invite her, she casually asked Nora if she
were going to the private view at the Academy,

which was to take place the day following
Lady Seaforth's visit.

"No, but I would like to go," answered
Nora; and then Lady Seaforth, in the interest
of her son, offered to take Nora; and Nora
felt, therefore, that if she accepted this kindness
from her newly-found neighbour that she could
not very well decline to dine with her ladyship
the same evening, when she assured Nora that
they would be *quite alone.*

"I know you will not care to meet any one
just yet," said Lady Seaforth, in her calm,
gracious way; "but if you will take pity upon
an invalid like myself, for I am far from
well to-day, and dine with me this evening,
I shall be very pleased. I fear my son is
engaged, or I should have asked him, but he
told me he was going somewhere or other."

Nora accepted this invitation. But when
she entered Lady Seaforth's drawing-room,
dressed in her deep mourning, a tall, slim,
graceful young man rose to receive her as well
as Lady Seaforth.

"Permit me to present my son to you," said
Lady Seaforth. "Seaforth, this is Mrs. Trelawn."

Nora bowed and smiled. She knew this

young lord very well by sight. She had seen
him as a gay and handsome boy, and she had
seen him when his gaiety had all passed away,
and when his face had grown worn, cynical,
and sad.

But she spoke to him now for the first time,
and she spoke to him with the ease and sweetness which made one of her charms. She was
indeed glad to know him, and though she was
only his own age she somehow regarded him
as very much younger than herself. She was
one of those women who can feel perfectly
friendly with a man without feeling the re-
motest wish to attract his admiration or peculiar
regard. So before the well-served dinner
which followed was over, Lord Seaforth had
made up his mind that Crœsus's widow was
charming, that she was a dear little woman,
and that if she hadn't a penny, a man might be
glad to win her, and make her his wife.

The mother looked on well pleased. She
saw her son was interested and amused, and
she gladly watched the old sweet boyish smile
that she now so seldom saw steal over his lips.

" He may learn even to love her," she
thought, wistfully, later on during the evening.

But when the evening was over, Lord Seaforth, having escorted Mrs. Trelawn to her house next door, went back to his mother's drawing-room, and the shadow which now his face so often wore had once more returned to it.

"Well, what do you think of her?" asked Lady Seaforth.

The young man laughed, and shrugged his shoulders.

"She's too nice a woman for me to think of," he said. "Not the style, in fact. I want something that wouldn't cost so much—something or someone who wouldn't expect so much. No, Crœsus's charming widow won't do for me!"

"What nonsense," said his mother.

"Sad fact," answered the young lord. And then he went to his club, and in his careless, thoughtless fashion told some of his chums when he got there about "Crœsus's Widow."

Thus the name was given to her. When Nora went the next day to the private view at the Academy, people looked after her, and at her, as they had never looked before. It began to be whispered, in fact, that the young widow with Lady Seaforth was about the richest

independent woman in London. Lady Seaforth's motive for appearing with her in public
was, of course, well understood. Other dowagers
with spendthrift sons sighed enviously when
they saw the young lord join his mother and
Nora, and saw the soft blush on the rich
widow's cheeks as she listened smilingly to the
young lord's cynical and often bitter criticisms
on those around him.

"You wish to destroy my illusions, I see,
about the 'world of beauty and fashion,'" said
Nora, with some archness of manner, in answer
to one of these remarks.

"The 'world of beauty and fashion' destroyed
all my illusions some years ago," said Lord
Seaforth. "Would you believe it, Mrs. Trelawn, I was once the most amiable, believing,
and gushing of young men!"

Nora laughed.

"I remember you," she said, "a bright-faced
boy."

Seaforth laughed also.

"That bright face," he said, "was the indi-
cator of the brightness within. I was a jolly
boy, wasn't I, mother?"

Lady Seaforth answered with a sigh.

"I hope you will yet live to be a happy man, Seaforth," she said.

Seaforth shrugged his shoulders.

"You hope that I'll be a very rare specimen of my race, then, mother," he answered. "Happiness after a certain age is, in my opinion, unattainable. What do you say, Mrs. Trelawn? Do you believe that either men or women are ever happy after twenty?"

For a moment Nora was silent. Her memory went back to the few bright days of her own life, which had all been before *she* was twenty. She saw again, at that instant, the handsome painter's face; and the evening haze, rising from the meadows as it had done in the brief hours of her love dream, when her soul had been absolutely flooded with happiness and hope.

Her face softened, and some of its girlish charm came back to it as this vision of byegone hours passed before her. For a minute or two she looked so like the Nora Sudely of old, that a man who was watching her almost started, and his heart began to throb as it had not throbbed for years.

This man was Walter Vyner—W. D. Vyner,

the famous painter now—the lover who had
stood hand-in-hand with Nora in the Warbrooke
meadows long ago, and who had just learned
that she was a widow; that all John Trelawn's
vast wealth had come to the dark-eyed girl
whose love had once been his.

The painter stood still, watching Nora. He
saw her smile on the young lord by her side,.
and he heard some lady whisper, "It is a good
thing for Seaforth."

But, almost as he heard that whisper, Nora's
eyes fell on the fine face which had seemed so
perfect to her girlish fancy. She visibly started
as she recognised Vyner, and the painter saw
the flush that rose to her cheeks as she bowed
to him and moved forward so as to take his
hand.

"You are in town, then," said Vyner, with
some embarrassment.

"Yes," answered Nora. And then she added,
softly, "You must come and see me, Mr. Vyner;
my aunt, Lady Stainbrooke, is with me."

"I bear that old lady no love," said the
painter, and his expression changed as he spoke,
"but—I shall be glad to call upon you."

"Do come," said Nora; and then, remem-

bering that she was walking with Lord Seaforth,
she introduced the painter to him.

The two men bowed coldly; and Vyner bit
his lips, and Lord Seaforth's pale face slightly
flushed as she did so.

"I have already had the honour of an introduction to—this gentleman, I think," said
Vyner, in anything but an agreeable tone of
voice.

"Yes—I have met Mr. Vyner," said Seaforth,
with a certain discomfort in his manner, which
was very unusual with him.

Scarcely anything more was said. Vyner
took off his hat and passed on with a frown
upon his brow and an angry feeling in his
heart. Yet he did not leave the room where
Nora was. He stood looking at her from a
distance—looking at her and thinking regret-
fully of the past.

"It's the old sweet face," he thought; "the
sweet, trustful, honest face which would have
kept me straight all my life if I'd had the luck
to win it. But now—what is the use of going
near her again—now, when it's too late."

He made an impatient gesture, and the
frown deepened upon his forehead as the last

reflection passed through his mind. Too late ?
and yet Nora's dark eyes had brightened and
her cheeks flushed a welcome when her little
hand was clasped in his!

In the meanwhile Lord Seaforth was still
walking with his mother and Mrs. Trelawn.
But the young lord's manner had changed
somewhat since that brief interview with the
painter. He was silent for some minutes after
they parted with Vyner, and then almost
abruptly he said to Nora—

"So you know Vyner, the painter, do you?
Have you known him long?"

"Yes, for years," answered Nora, gravely.
"I knew Mr. Vyner before my marriage."

"Indeed!" said Lord Seaforth, as if surprised.
Then he added, after a moment's thought,
"But of late years I suppose—you know nothing
or little about him—except as a painter?"

"I have been proud of him," said Nora, and
her dark eyes sparkled; "proud of the old friend
who has won the fame that he once dreamed
of—who—who is now what he hoped to be—
when I knew him as a girl."

Seaforth made no reply to this. But he
grew so absent in manner that Lady Seaforth

proposed to Nora that they should leave the Academy. Lady Seaforth was afraid of wearying her beloved son of the lady whom she wished to be his wife !

Seaforth escorted his mother and Nora to their carriage, and then called a hansom and drove straight to one of the entrances to Regent's Park. There he dismissed his hansom, and proceeded direct to a seat under the shadow of some trees, where he expected a friend would be waiting for him.

This friend was waiting for him—a young girl fair to look upon—who started up with a glad smile of welcome on her rosy lips as he drew near.

"Well, Miss Nellie," he said, holding out his hand, "I hope I have not kept you waiting ?"

"Indeed you have," answered "Miss Nellie," still smiling. "I have not the honour of possessing a watch, you know, but I think it must be a little past four now."

Seaforth looked at his watch, and then gave a sort of impatient sigh.

"It is past five, my poor Nellie," he said, "but I really could not come before. I took my mother to the private view of the Academy, and who do you think I saw there, Nellie?"

The girl shook her head. She was looking up in his face—looking as women look on the faces they love.

"How can I tell?" she said.

"Vyner, the painter," continued Seaforth. "He spoke to a lady who was with my mother—and, little Nellie—something leaked out, you know" (and Seaforth took the girl's hand, and drew her down on the seat from which she had risen when he approached her), "something which perhaps I ought to have told you before — only it seemed no matter."

"What is it, Captain Seaforth?" asked "Miss Nellie," and her colour faded a little as she spoke.

"Only a little, little thing, Nellie," answered Lord Seaforth, "and really no earthly consequence to us. But lest at any future time you should think me a liar or a gay deceiver, I ought, perhaps, to tell you that my honourable and respected parent, now lying in his grave— who ruined me before he retired to it, by-the-bye—was one of that order whom a certain Tommy is said to have loved."

"Miss Nellie" looked up as if she did not understand all this.

"To explain more fully," continued Lord Seaforth, "I have the misfortune to be, Nellie—well, for one thing, little better than a beggar."

"Oh! I'm so sorry, so sorry," said Nellie, and she nestled her little hand more closely into his, and looked at him with sweet, wistful eyes. "But—but, this will make no difference to me?"

"Won't it, though?" answered Lord Seaforth, trying to speak lightly. "All women, you know, love the gauds of this world—and you are a little woman, I suppose, like the rest?"

"Not like the rest if they care for money more—more than—"

"More than love, do you mean, child? So you care for love most of all, Nellie—*really* most of all?"

"Yes," half-whispered the girl, and she coloured all over her fine soft skin.

"And you love me—a worthless fellow like me? Ah, Nellie, you are a foolish, foolish little girl!"

"Do you mean because you are poor ?" asked Nellie, yet more wistfully.

"Because I am poor, and because I am worthless, and because I have not even told you the truth, Nellie, about my position in life," answered Lord Seaforth.

"How do you mean ? Please tell me what you mean ?"

"Vyner, the painter, will tell you—will tell your sister most likely to-day, that I have been sailing under false colours. Don't look so frightened, Nellie—it's nothing awful I have to relate—simply that instead of being Captain Seaforth, as you have known me, I am Lord Seaforth ; and Vyner heard my title to-day."

"Lord Seaforth !" repeated Nellie, and she started up, turned quite pale, and stood looking in the young lord's face.

"At your service—but you don't seem to like the new name, Nellie, as well as the old ?"

"No, no, no !" exclaimed the girl, and she put out her hands with a gesture of pain and anger. "Now I know what you mean —I am foolish to care for you, you think—when, when we are so far apart ?" And she burst into passionate tears.

"Nay, nonsense, Nellie!" said Lord Seaforth, and he also rose, and put his arm around
her. "Hush, child, darling, do not tremble
so—we will talk it over—we will see what we
can do—only don't distress yourself; don't
·cry, my dear, dear little Nell."

CHAPTER V.

NELLIE.

BEFORE the interview between Lord Seaforth and "Miss Nellie" ended, Lord Seaforth had persuaded her to forgive him for having deceived her, or rather allowed her to deceive herself, about his name.

The error into which she had fallen was very easily accounted for. One morning "Miss Nellie" and her dog, a handsome collie, were crossing the roadway near St. George's Hospital, when the unfortunate collie was knocked down and run over by a hansom cab. The young man seated in the cab heard the girl's shriek, as she saw what had happened, and he at once jumped out, and helped to lift the poor dog up, and carried it to its young mistress, who, forgetting everything but her favourite's sufferings, knelt down on the pavement, and laid the poor brute's head tenderly on her lap.

" I am so very, very sorry," said the young
man (Lord Seaforth), "but I fear the dog is
done for, and if you will allow me I'll get him
taken away, and put an end to him at once."

Then the girl (Miss Nellie) looked up indignantly, and Lord Seaforth saw how pretty
she was.

" Do you mean take him away to be killed?"
said "Miss Nellie." "Kill my poor, poor
man" (and she once more bent over the injured
dog, who looked up in her face, and tried to.
lick her hand) "because he is hurt? You shall
not do that, sir! I will never leave Wallace,
and he shall never leave me whilst he is alive."

" I am truly sorry," again said Lord Seaforth.
" Shall I call a cab, then, and drive you home
with your dog?"

" If you will do that I shall be very much
obliged," answered the girl, who was beginning
to be aware that she was fast becoming the
centre of a crowd.

So Lord Seaforth called a four-wheeled cab,
and poor Wallace was lifted into it, and held
partly in "Miss Nellie's" arms, and partly in
Lord Seaforth's, until they reached the small
house in the small street near Regent's Park,

where "Miss Nellie" informed Lord Seaforth that her father, Major Blythe, then lived.

Nellie got out of the cab, and ran into the house first to break the news of the dog's accident to her father.

"For he is blind," she said to Lord Seaforth, "and that, of course, makes us love him and think of him more."

Lord Seaforth smiled a grim smile at the situation he found himself in, after the girl left him. Sitting in a cab, nursing a strange dog! But he felt repaid when "Miss Nellie" reappeared, leading her blind father by the hand.

"This is my father, Major Blythe," said Nellie, "I—I do not know your name—but he has been so kind to dear Wallace, father."

"My name is Seaforth," answered Lord Seaforth, getting out of the cab and smiling. "I am glad to make the acquaintance of Major Blythe—for I, too, am a soldier."

"Thank you for your kindness to my little girl," said Major Blythe, "and to the poor dog, who is an old and faithful friend to us all. Will you come in—Mr.—or are you Captain Seaforth?"

"I hold a captain's commission," answered

Lord Seaforth, looking with some interest at
the blind Major.

He saw a tall, grey-haired man, with a noble
face, and an expression of almost touching
resignation. This was the pretty girl's father,
then—the pretty girl who, when Lord Seaforth
looked round for her, was lifting out her injured
dog from the cab, and speaking to it in tones
of sympathising endearment.

They carried it together—Lord Seaforth and
Nellie—into the meagrely-furnished parlour
close to the house door, and Nellie went down
on her knees and made poor Wallace a bed
with a simple grace that the young man could
not but admire.

She was pretty—not a regular beauty, though
with perfect features—but it was a face with
a charm. Modest, innocent, and sweet, with
bright, light, curly, ruffled air, and a fair,
smooth, fresh, rosy, girlish skin.

"She is a little rosebud," thought Lord
Seaforth ; and as he assisted her to make the
dog's bed, he determined not to lose sight of
"Miss Nellie."

"Let me bring you a 'vet' to see Wallace,"
he said. "I know a very clever fellow who

belongs to us and he'll do what he can for the dog."

Lord Seaforth brought the "vet," and Wallace was nursed and tended until he was "the happiest dog alive," Seaforth told Nellie. Seaforth came very often to inquire after the dog, and sat in the little parlour and talked to the blind Major, and looked at the golden head of "Miss Nellie."

He called her "Miss Nellie" in these days. She was the Major's youngest daughter, and Miss Blythe—Margaret, the eldest—was from home. Seaforth soon learnt all the little simple family history. Major Blythe had been in an infantry regiment, and his sight had been affected by a sunstroke in India. Then he had left the regular army, and had become an adjutant to a militia corps. But he gradually grew blind. They were terrible hours, he told Lord Seaforth in his simple way, when he first knew that his sight was doomed.

"*She* was my little comforter," he said, softly, laying his hand on Nellie's fair, ruffled, curly air, and the girl looked up and put her arms round her blind father's neck.

"I said I would be his spectacles!" she said, trying to speak lightly, but Seaforth saw her blue eyes grow moist, and the next moment she dashed away a tear.

A very tender love existed between the father and daughter. Major Blythe admitted to Seaforth that she was his darling, though "Margaret, my eldest daughter, is a most excellent, clever woman," the old soldier told his visitor; "but, then, Margaret is ten years older than Nellie, and so naturally Nellie is the spoilt darling of the household."

"The spoilt darling of the household," however, showed very few signs of being spoilt. She was a bright, sweet, unselfish girl, with a little hot temper, perhaps, sometimes, but the moment it was over it was gone for ever. No one ever saw a frown or a sulky look on Nellie Blythe's fair face.

"She is like the sunshine," said her fond father, and soon Seaforth did not care to tell or think how much he thought of Nellie Blythe.

Their acquaintance went on very smoothly and pleasantly at first. Then Margaret Blythe returned home, and she shook her head and looked very grave when she heard about "Captain Seaforth."

"It is unwise to allow him to come here,

father," she said to the Major. "He is in the Guards, you say, and altogether an unsuitable acquaintance for Nellie."

Margaret Blythe was quite different in appearance to Nellie, but she also was good-looking. She was tall and dark, and very determined, and she was a professional artist, and an illustrator of books when she could get employment. During her meritorious struggles (for the Blythes were very poor) Margaret had made the acquaintance of W. D. Vyner, the painter. The woman usually so cold and self-contained was not cold to the handsome artist. She admired him, and she grew fond and proud of him. Vyner was lonely, and not particularly happy, and he liked and respected Margaret Blythe, and he had drifted into an engagement with her. They had been engaged six months when he saw again the face of his first love at the Academy—when he learned that Nora Trelawn was free—that rich John Trelawn was dead, and that all his great wealth had come to his young widow.

Vyner had once met Lord Seaforth at the Blythes, and had been introduced to him as "Captain Seaforth." But Seaforth only went very rarely to the Blythes' house now. Margaret had given him to understand that he was not a very welcome visitor to her, and Seaforth—perhaps gladly—had taken advantage of this intimation to induce his friend Nellie to meet him unknown to her sister. They had met each other, and walked together many and many a time before Lord Seaforth had been urged by his mother to think of Nora Trelawn; before his own overwhelming embarrassments had often made him resolve to break with sweet Nellie Blythe.

But this was not an easy thing to the young man's heart. His wild and reckless life had grown wearisome to him, and the women on whom he had wasted his substance had palled upon him, but it was too late. Lord Seaforth was a ruined man, and what Lady Seaforth had told him was but too true. Unless he married a woman with a great fortune his career was ended. And yet still he did not care to break sweet Nellie's heart; for he believed that the girl loved him. Her soft, innocent eyes had betrayed this a hundred times, and though no binding words had absolutely passed between them, Seaforth knew that in honour he was bound to Nellie.

CHAPTER VI.

MARGARET.

HE did not accompany her home after he had told her that his real name was Murray, Viscount Seaforth, and that he was little better than a beggar. He left her at the Metropolitan Railway Station, which was almost close to the street in which Major Blythe lived, and then Nellie went on thoughtfully to her father's house.

The street door was opened as she approached it, and her eldest sister stood there looking anxiously out.

"Nellie, where have you been ? " she said. "How late you are."

"Only sitting in the park," answered Nellie, while the tell-tale colour flushed through her fair skin.

"'Tis too late for a young girl like you to

sit in the park alone," answered Margaret.
" Have you brought in father's paper ? "

" Oh !—I've forgotten !" exclaimed Nellie,
in real distress.

" It is thoughtless and unkind of you," said
Margaret, " when he has so few pleasures, and
he has asked for it twice. I should have gone
for it myself, but I dare not leave Hatton in
the house alone for fear she sets it on fire."

"I will run and get the paper now, Margaret."

" No, I will get it. But Nellie, come in here;
I have got something to tell you." And
the elder sister drew the younger one into a
little back room, and closed the door behind
them.

" Walter Vyner has been here," began Margaret, " and he has just been telling me a
shameful thing, Nellie."

" What has he been telling you ? " said
Nellie, quickly.

" That Captain Seaforth, whom you and my
father think so much of, is actually not Captain
Seaforth," continued Margaret. " Walter saw
him at the private view at the Academy to-day
with a lady whom he knew long ago, and this
lady was with Lady Seaforth, and the man

who has passed himself off here as Captain Seaforth is really Lord Seaforth! I call it exceedingly insulting to us."

For a moment Nellie was silent. Her delicate skin flushed, and her lips trembled; then she said sharply, almost defiantly—

"Yes, I know."

"You knew, absolutely knew, that a man was coming to your father's house under a false title, and never told it! Then I'm ashamed of you," exclaimed Margaret, very angrily.

"Very well, you can be ashamed," retorted Nellie, her quick temper asserting itself.

"When did he let you know this?" said Margaret, scornfully. "After he was found out to-day, I suppose, when he knew it was no use trying to deceive us any longer?"

Nellie bit her lips and did not speak.

"Can you not see through his motives for this?" proceeded Margaret. "He meant to amuse himself with a silly girl, and whenever anything serious might be expected to come of it he intended to vanish! There is, indeed, no Captain Seaforth, and *Lord* Seaforth has throughout acted in a most ungentlemanly manner."

"The mistake arose through me," said Nellie. "When he came here first—and you know how that happened—I said, 'I do not know your name,' and he simply said, 'My name is Seaforth:' and it is 'Seaforth.' What deception was there in that? Perhaps he did not care to tell us he was a lord when we were living in a little house like this. It was from delicacy of feeling, Margaret, and not from any wish to deceive. Then father said—Was he Mr. or Captain Seaforth (never, of course, guessing his real rank), and he said, 'I hold a captain's commission'; and he does hold a captain's commission. There! What lie did he tell? You are unjust, Margaret; and I think Mr. Vyner need not have come here to make mischief."

Nellie had talked till she was quite hot and red. She stood there facing her sister and defending her lover with sparkling eyes and quivering lips, a true type of womanhood! The man had erred, and the woman having herself forgiven him, would not permit another to disparage him.

"It is all very fine to talk thus," again commenced Margaret; but at this point her

words were interrupted by an unkempt red
head—on which was perched a very funny
looking cap—being thrust in at the door.

"Miss Blythe, please, master's howling for
his papers," said the owner of the head and the
cap.

"What an expression, Hatton! Why do
you use such words as howling?" said Margaret,
reprovingly.

"Isn't it right," asked Hatton, and she put
the thumb of her left hand on her hip, and
stood looking contemplatively at her mistress.

She was a most comical figure; all angles,
even the eyes being oblique of vision. She
was the only handmaiden of the Blythe family,
and Margaret tried in vain to make her pre-
sentable. She insisted for one thing on calling
her "Hatton," though "Becky" had been the
name that this waif of the streets had gone by
since her cradle in the dust-pan.

"But," Margaret Blythe had told her, "in all
good families the female servants bear their
surnames."

"And this is a 'good family?'" said Becky,
with a sly look in the oblique eyes. "Oh, please,
miss, I didn't know it."

Margaret could not help smiling at this, though still she insisted upon "Becky" being called Hatton, but the change of name did not change the girl. "Hatton" remained hopelessly comical and absurd-looking, and was a constant eyesore to Margaret's artistic tastes. But Hatton knew how to work.

"I've been at it ever since I was put down," she once told Nellie, "and my legs got that bowed with being put down and working too soon, that they've kept on that way inclined."

This odd-looking damsel now stood looking at the sisters, with her thumb upon her hip.

"What have I to say to master, miss, when he yells out again for the papers?" she said, presently.

"Say I will get them for him. Miss Nellie has forgotten them," answered Margaret. And Miss Nellie took advantage of this break in the discussion with her sister, and as Hatton turned to leave the room she left it also, and went to seek her blind father.

"Father, I have been so naughty," she said, going up to the Major and slipping her little hand into his. "I forgot to get your paper."

"Well, my little girl, never mind; Hatton will get me one, and then you'll read it to me," he answered, stroking her small hand.

"And father, have you heard, has Margaret told you, what a stupid mistake we have both made?" And the Major felt the small hand twitch.

"No, darling. I've hardly seen Margaret to-day. Vyner has been here, and she has been talking to him."

"I know. Well, it seems, father, we have made such a silly mistake. Don't you remember the first time—when Wallace was hurt, you know—how we asked somebody his name, and he said it was Seaforth?"

"Yes, darling, of course—Captain Seaforth."

"He never said *Captain* Seaforth," continued Nellie; "he just said 'Seaforth, and that he held a captain's commission. Well, he is Seaforth, and he does hold a captain's commission—but, father, he has another title, too—and he told me this to-day."

"Have you seen Captain Seaforth to-day, Nellie?" asked the Major, with just a shade of anxiety in his tone.

"Yes; I met him, and he said he had something to tell me," answered Nellie, bravely. "And what do you think this something is, father? He is really Lord Seaforth."

"Lord Seaforth!" repeated the Major. "You indeed surprise me, Nellie."

"Yes, isn't it a surprise?" said Nellie, trying to speak lightly. "We have been entertaining, not an angel, but a lord unawares, it seems. And Margaret has been so stupid about it, father! She has been scolding me, and talking all sorts of nonsense, just as if he could have any motive for deceiving us—it is so silly of Margaret."

The Major was silent for a moment or two, then he said—

"I wish this young man had told us this before, Nellie."

"But why, father? Isn't he just the same? He is a gentleman, and you are a gentleman. What matters it whether he is Captain or Lord Seaforth?"

"The world would say it was a good deal of matter, Nellie. Rank, like money, makes a distinct difference of class. It was not right of Lord Seaforth to allow us to go on calling him Captain Seaforth."

"Now, father, you are just as horrid as Margaret," said the "spoilt darling of the household," and she put her arm fondly round her kind father's neck. "Don't you begin scolding too, dear old man, or I'll have a fine life between you! Promise me one thing, father, that when he—when Lord Seaforth comes—that you will be quite kind to him, for you must not forget how kind he has been to us—and to the dear old doggie, too!" and Nellie stroked the lame collie's head, for Wallace was sitting, as usual, at his master's feet, looking up with his soft, wistful, brown eyes, into that patient face.

CHAPTER VII.

THE OLD LOVE.

WALTER VYNEE kept his promise, and went to call upon his old love, Nora Trelawn, a few days after he had met her at the private view at the Academy.

Nora Trelawn was very rich, and she was also a woman of taste ; and lately she had taken some pleasure and interest in the furnishing and adornment of her house ; and Vyner saw all this, as he stood a moment or two alone in her drawing-room, and he saw also on the soft-tinted walls two pictures of his own, which had been purchased through a dealer, and for which Nora had given a great price.

Vyner stood still, looking at his pictures thoughtfully, as we sometimes look at our own work. Perhaps he was not thinking only of his pictures—a dark-eyed girl, in the hazy

meadows in the eventide, was standing shadow-
like before him, also in his mental vision. But
his contemplation of the real and the ideal was
speedily interrupted. A lady, not knowing he
was there, now entered the room; and sat
down on the first couch she came to, panting,
and fanning herself.

Vyner turned round and looked at her. It
was Lady Stainbrooke, Nora's aunt—Lady
Stainbrooke, a little browner and more
wrinkled than she was five years ago, but
otherwise not much altered. Vyner knew her
again at once. He remembered at that moment
the lie she had told Nora—the lie which had
parted him from the girl he loved.

He made a slight movement, and Lady
Stainbrooke looked up and saw him.

"Is that you, Mr. Vyner?" she said. "He
is looking after Nora's money," she thought.

Vyner bowed a cold and stately bow, but the
old lady held out a withered hand, and looked
at Vyner with involuntary admiration.

What had the five years done for the
handsome painter? His face was darker and
graver, but he was handsome still. The
sharply-cut features, the bright grey eyes, were

unchanged ; but the expression of the classic
mouth was altered. The enthusiasm, the
passion of youth, had passed away ; and a
calm—almost a proud—look of composure had
replaced them. The man had gone into the
arena, and fought and conquered. W. D.
Vyner's name was known now all over Europe,
and as Lady Stainbrooke looked at him
admiringly, with her sharp, brown eyes, she
remembered this.

"So," she said, smiling, and still fanning
herself, "you are a great man now, Mr. Vyner.
Well, I prophesied you would be, long ago, if
you remember."

Vyner, who was a hater of shams, answered
with more abruptness than politeness.

"I thought it was exactly the other way,
Lady Stainbrooke," he said.

The old lady laughed, and showed her yellow
teeth.

"Ah," she said, "I recollect that day, Mr.
Vyner, when you fancied I was speaking about
one of your pictures to my niece, Nora, but in
reality I was alluding to some other artist. To
be sure, it seems like yesterday, and yet it is
five or six years ago, for it was just at the time

when Nora was first engaged to poor, dear John
Trelawn. You will have heard, I suppose, that
he is dead, and that he has left a great fortune
to Nora? Ah! all the men are after her now,
Mr. Vyner," and the old lady laughed again,
enjoying her delicate little stab.

Vyner made no answer. He stood looking
at Lady Stainbrooke with a half-scornful
smile, for he knew that he at least could not
be accused of seeking Nora for her money.

"I do not blame people in the least,"
continued Lady Stainbrooke in her jaunty,
rather humorous way, "for paying court to
the rich, for they are so much pleasanter
acquaintances than the poor! One can never
be quite sure indeed that a poor friend isn't
going to ask for the loan of a five-pound note.
And then the wealthy have so much in their
power—even you great artists, Mr. Vyner, want
patrons, you know!"

"Yes," answered Vyner, bitterly, "we sell
our work, Lady Stainbrooke, as you ladies sell
your faces."

Lady Stainbrooke nodded her head and
fanned herself more vigorously than ever.

"Not bad," she said, approvingly. "So we

do sell our faces, Mr. Vyner, and therefore beauty is a great gift. Where should I have been now, I wonder, if I had not been a pretty girl—though perhaps you are surprised to hear I ever was? And where would Nora have been if she had not sold her face to poor dear John Trelawn? She would not have had young Lord Seaforth at her feet, as she has now, I promise you."

"She might have been a happier woman," said Vyner, gravely; and as he spoke the room door opened, and Nora herself walked in.

There was a glad light in her eyes, and a pink flush in her soft cheeks, and she held out her hand frankly and cordially.

"I am glad to see you, Mr. Vyner," she said. I—I—have been expecting you to call."

"I intended to come yesterday," said Vyner, "but a man's time is not always his own."

"A lady in the way, eh, Mr. Vyner?" asked Lady Stainbrooke.

"You are fond of inventing ladies for my benefit, it seems, Lady Stainbrooke," answered Vyner, very grimly.

Lady Stainbrooke looked up at this sharply, and glanced from Nora to Vyner. She

knew, or rather guessed, at that moment that
some sort of explanation must have passed
between them before John Trelawn's death, but
she was too shrewd to remark upon this.

"I have been complimenting Mr. Vyner on
his success, my dear," she said, turning to
Nora.

"Yes," said Nora; "I have been pleased
—and proud."

Her voice faltered a little as she uttered the
two last words, and she cast down her dark eyes;
and Vyner's voice also showed some emotion
when he spoke.

"I see," he said, smiling, and with a sort of
gesture towards his pictures hanging on the
wall, "that you have been one of the patrons
whom Lady Stainbrooke has just been telling
me that we artists are obliged to court."

"Ah, Mr. Vyner, Mr. Vyner, that is a little
too bad!" laughed Lady Stainbrooke, with a
slightly-forced laugh, for she did not wish to
offend her rich niece Nora. "I said nothing
of the kind, my dear; but I see, I see!" And
Lady Stainbrooke nodded her head after her
usual fashion.

"Well, what do you see, aunt?" asked Nora.

" Mr. Vyner is too great a man now to like my little innocent jests—ah, yes, that is just the way—success is very trying, Mr. Vyner."

" Do you mean to the temper, Lady Stainbrooke ?" asked Vyner.

" To the temper and the disposition," answered her ladyship, agreeably. " It requires a strong head not to be turned by adulation."

" Mine has had no chance of being turned, then," said Vyner.

" Ah, ah, so you tell us," said Lady Stainbrooke, " but perhaps we know better. Nora, my love, don't you expect Lady Seaforth this afternoon ?"

" She said something about coming in to see the new pattern I got at the Art School yesterday," replied Nora. " But it is no matter," she added indifferently.

" If I am in the way——" said Vyner, rising, and understanding Lady Stainbrooke's hint.

" But you are not in the way," said Nora, softly, and she looked smilingly at Vyner.

" I am glad of that," he answered, " for it is pleasant to see the face of an old friend."

" And a patron too!" said Lady Stainbrooke, with a little scoffing laugh.

She was a worldly old woman this, and put little trust in men, and less in women. She knew the world, she thought, and the hearts of those who live in it; but she measured these hearts by her own narrow gauge. It was but natural that she should suppose that Walter Vyner had come to court Nora for her wealth, for she spent a good deal of time in courting Nora herself. There are feelings and motives that Lady Stainbrooke did not understand, and therefore she did not believe in them. She understood, however—as we have seen— the power of money; and she esteemed it above all earthly, or, alas, heavenly things!

But Vyner was not afraid of Lady Stainbrooke's sharp tongue. He stood there looking at his old friend, and he was not thinking of her as a wealthy widow, but as the bright girl he had loved long years ago. The shadow of these years—which at one time had changed Nora's face so much—at this moment seemed quite passed away. She, also, was thinking of her maiden days, and of the lover to whom she had given her young heart. And this lover was before her now. No chill poverty to part them now—nothing to part them—thought

Nora Trelawn, as she smiled softly, and looked on Vyner's face.

But presently Vyner gave a short, impatient sigh, a jerk almost of the grandly-shaped head. A memory had flitted across his mind. A woman good, true, and handsome—handsome, and yet without the nameless charm which makes true beauty—had risen before his mental vision, and stood there cold and shadow-like before Nora. To this woman he was bound in honour he remembered, and so he averted his eyes from the sweet attractive face of his first, nay his only love.

Nora noticed his change of expression, but she never thought of any other woman in the way

"Is this good?" she said, smiling and pointing to a costly vase which she had recently purchased. "I am never quite sure, you know, Mr. Vyner, whether my taste is good or bad."

Again Vyner thought of Margaret Blythe as Nora said these simple words. Margaret was quite sure about *her* taste. She thought she had the best taste in the world, and was fond of announcing this, and giving very decided advice upon all occasions.

"A little girl I once knew," said Vyner, with an involuntary ring of tenderness in his voice, "used to have a very pretty taste of her own, if I remember right, in the way of dresses and bonnets, etc., and that is, I think, the best criterion of a woman's taste. I hate an ill-dressed woman!"

"Quite right, Mr. Vyner," said old Lady Stainbrooke, blinking behind her glasses; "a well-dressed woman always looks well—but ah!—ah, it costs money," and she sighed, and moved her lean, wrinkled hands, for she was very avaricious, and hated to open her purse-strings even for her own adornment.

At this moment an exceedingly well-dressed woman was ushered into Nora's drawing-room. This was her next-door neighbour, Lady Seaforth, who, in the interest of her son, was now very attentive to Nora.

But she forwarded this interest so gracefully, and with such well-bred ease, that Nora could not help liking her. Lady Seaforth was a handsome woman, with all the advantages of high caste to add to her attractions. The dust of the earth came not near her, and the stock from which she sprang for generations had been

unmarred by labour. She was a haughty
woman, but she wanted money, and so she
bowed her proud head and went to Nora's.
Nora personally she rather liked, but Lady
Stainbrooke was an eyesore and an obstruction,
the patrician dame decided, whenever she
contemplated Nora's marriage with her son.

She sometimes affected—still in her patrician
way—the society of people of talent. They
were gifted, she thought, and so they ought
to be cultivated. But in her heart she looked
down upon the giants towering above their
fellows, unless blue blood ran through their
veins. Her grace and culture of manner,
however, prevented this being visible.

" I am pleased to make Mr. Vyner's
acquaintance," she said, when Nora had
presented the painter to her. " I have long
known and admired his work."

Vyner bowed, and took the compliment very
quietly. He was past the stage when praise is
so sweet, and recognition dearer than the
breath of life. He had his pride too, but not
the pride of birth, yet of his birthright. He had
not been born with a great name, but with the
genius to make one. He was greater than

Alice Elizabeth, Viscountess Seaforth, whatever
her ladyship might think. Alice Elizabeth,
Viscountess Seaforth, would die and be buried,
and have her title carved on her gravestone,
and there would be an end of her; but Vyner's
hand had carved a name that would not die,
and done work that would live as long as his
canvass hung together.

So he did not bow very humbly to my lady.
But my lady was very gracious.

Mr. Vyner must dine with her some day
soon, she said; and again Vyner bowed, and
wondered if he would meet his old friend, his
dark-eyed Nora, at Lady Seaforth's.

Then he went away, and the image of his
dark-eyed Nora went with him.

"She is my Eve," he said, pacing backwards
and forwards in his studio, with his long strides,
as the daylight faded. "God made her for me
just as He made the first woman for the first man.
She is part of me, and yet we are separated—
ay, I know it well—by a promise I cannot break."

Yet that night he commenced a picture—it
was his Eve as she stood in the Warbrooke
meadows long ago, in her bright maidenhood,
before the shadows had fallen upon her face.

CHAPTER VIII.

HIS EVE.

THE man loved his work, and it throve and prospered under his hand.

"This promises to be a fine picture," said his betrothed, Margaret Blythe, to the painter one day, when she had unexpectedly visited his studio, pausing before an unfinished sketch of a dark-eyed woman. "What do you mean to call it?"

"I call it 'My Eve,'" answered Vyner, gravely regarding his own work.

"'My Eve!'" repeated Margaret. "What an extraordinary name—I am sure I could think of a much better one."

"Not for this picture," said Vyner.

"Yes, I am sure I could," replied Margaret, for she believed that no one could do anything so well as herself. "Fancy a dark Eve—of course, Eve was fair."

"Why?" asked Vyner, smiling. "Besides, this may not be intended for the lady who brought such trouble and toil upon us all." And Vyner gave rather a weary sigh.

"We make our own troubles very often," said Margaret.

"I dare say," said Vyner, indifferently, for he was not thinking of Margaret, nor of her correct and proper ways.

Margaret thought herself a paragon among women, and indeed she might be one, but it is sometimes a little wearisome to live with a self-conscious paragon. She had the most firm and simple faith in her own perfections. *Peccavi* was never heard on her lips. But she loved Vyner, and believed in him, though not as she believed in herself. He had genius, she thought, but she also had genius, only her devotion to her home duties prevented her gifts being recognised by the world.

Not the woman to touch Vyner's heart this!

There was a rugged honesty, truth and humility about this man; though he, too, believed in his own genius, counting it a gift from God. But he knew also of the dust stains—the follies, the passions, the meannesses—which

clung to and befouled his heart, as they cling
to and befoul the hearts of nearly all the erring
children of men.

Yet he tried to do right and walk straight,
and Margaret Blythe was satisfied with her
choice, and believed that Vyner was devoted
to her. She knew nothing about his Eve, but
if she had known it would scarcely have disturbed her equanimity. All men commit some
folly or other, Margaret Blythe thought, but
no "folly," she was sure, would change his
regard for the best and purest of women—
namely, for Margaret Blythe.

Yet as Margaret Blythe stood before the
picture of his Eve, he never before had fully
realised the bitterness of his bondage. Margaret—the woman whom he was engaged to
marry, and you sweet dark-eyed one, smiling
from his canvass ! Margaret, tall and slim, a
little angular about the shoulders, perhaps, but
handsome withal, and a model of all the virtues
personified !

And his Nora—his Eve—not beautiful, but
lovable, and pleasant to the eyes, and tender
and gentle to every living thing. The dumb
brutes crept to her protecting side, trusting her

with their God-given instinct, following her
with their mute and wistful eyes.

The painter recalled at this moment—his
living Margaret standing opposite to his
pictured Eve—when he had met Nora before
her husband's death, with the look of life-
weariness too plainly printed on her face. He
remembered the brief explanation which had
then passed between them—the words that
told the long, dull history of years.

"So," he had said, looking at John Trelawn's
wife, "that old woman spoilt two lives then?"

"She spoilt mine," Nora had answered in a
low tone; "but we must not speak of it now."

"And not even *now*," thought Vyner bitterly,
looking at his Margaret, and turning his eyes
away from his pictured Eve!

"Walter, will you come in this evening?"
said his Margaret, addressing him in her
measured tones.

"Not this evening, Margaret," answered
Vyner. "I am going to dine with Lady
Seaforth."

"With Lady Seaforth?" repeated Margaret,
surprised. "Do you know her then, Walter?
She is the mother, I suppose, of young Lord

Seaforth—the young man who forgot himself
so far, and forgot what was due to us so far, as
to come to our house without telling us his real
name?"

"Yes, she is his mother," said Vyner. "I
met her the other day, and she asked me to
dine with her this evening, and I accepted her
invitation."

"I am glad that you did, for I hope she will
call upon us when we are married."

Vyner shrugged his shoulders.

"She will have cut me most likely by that
time," he said. "These great ladies take one
up and drop one down just for a caprice,
Margaret. Don't marry me, please, for the
sake of visiting Lady Seaforth!"

"How foolish you are, Walter! No; but
really I wish you to cultivate good people—
people of position are so much more agreeable
than people without any."

"Precisely," said Vyner; "and so for this
laudable reason I am going to sacrifice myself,
and dine with her ladyship, instead of smoking
my pipe at home at my ease."

"I hope you will give up smoking when
you are married, Walter."

"Don't hope so then, Margaret; for I fear if you do it will end in disappointment—like visiting Lady Seaforth."

"I wonder if the young lord will say anything about *us* to-night?" continued Margaret. "He has never been to call lately—I can't quite find out—but I sometimes think that foolish child Nellie liked him?"

"I hope not," said Vyner, gravely. "I like little Nell, and would be sorry if any trouble came to her; and even among fast men, Margaret, Seaforth bears a bad reputation."

"I thought so," said Margaret, triumphantly. "Oh, I am never deceived; I was sure he was a bad man."

"Perhaps it is hard to call him so—he may but have been tempted beyond his strength. Which of us indeed has a right to fling the first or even the second stone, Margaret?"

"I do not agree with you, Walter. There are some, I hope, who live lives quite free of reproach. Since my earliest childhood, for instance, I have been devoted to my father and young sister—not that there is any great difference of age between Nellie and myself, but then my mind is more advanced than hers—

she is more childish; and as we were motherless, I felt it my duty to act as though I were very much older, and take entire charge of her."

There were ten years between the ages of the sisters, but these ten years were never alluded to at home. Margaret might be a paragon among women, but it was understood in the Blythe family that even paragons have their weaknesses, and that her age was Margaret Blythe's. Vyner, who thought that all women and all men have their weaknesses, only laughed in reply to Margaret's speech.

" Come, young lady," he said, "if I am to have the honour of escorting you home, we had better be starting ; for I must have time, you know, to wash the paint off before I appear at my Lady Seaforth's."

The painter walked home with his betrothed, and then returned to his rooms to dress. He had a feeling in his heart somehow that he was going to meet Nora Trelawn. And as his cab stopped at Lady Seaforth's door, one of Nora's footmen was just opening her door, and Nora herself, in soft black garments, came out, and stepped from her own portico to Lady Seaforth's, the big footman walking behind to carry her cloak.

She, of course, saw Vyner, and she blushed, and then looked the next moment brightly and gaily into his face. But her blush faded when she noticed the grave courtesy of his manner.

"We are to have the pleasure of dining together, then?" he said.

"Yes," answered Nora; and so together they entered the house, and were ushered into Lady Seaforth's drawing-room.

Lady Seaforth received them in the stately, gracious way which was natural to her. She was a woman who never allowed her feelings to influence her manner in society. She had been exceedingly annoyed just half-an-hour before Vyner and Nora appeared in her drawing-room, but now her smooth brow seemed quite unruffled.

The cause of her annoyance had been the beloved son. The beloved son had promised to dine with her; had promised to do his best to make himself agreeable to Crœsus's widow, and at the last moment had disappointed her. This had happened in a manner that seemed quite unaccountable to Lady Seaforth.

"Mr. Vyner, the painter, is going to dine

here as well," she said to her son, and Lord
Seaforth, who was actually leaving the room
for the purpose of dressing for dinner, made a
sudden pause.

"Vyner, the painter, mother! What on
earth induced you to ask him?" he said,
turning round and looking at Lady Seaforth.

"I met him at Mrs. Trelawn's," answered
his mother. "He is clever and presentable;
why should I not ask him, Seaforth?"

Lord Seaforth made no answer. He stood
there looking at his mother for a moment or
two as if he were undecided about something,
and then he looked at his watch.

"Mother," he said, "I am very sorry, but I
have forgotten something—I remember, now, I
can't dine here to-day; can't avail myself of the
chance of making love to Crœsus's fair or rather
dark widow—I have an engagement I can't get
off."

Lady Seaforth was seriously annoyed, nay
angry, with her son.

"What reason have you for making this
excuse?" she said.

"My unfortunate memory," answered Lord
Seaforth, in his careless, mocking way. "I am

truly sorry—pray give my best regards to
Madam Crœsus."

"How can you act thus—how can you speak
thus—when you know the bitter necessity for
this step?" said Lady Seaforth.

Her son shrugged his shoulders.

"I will see her some other day," he said,
"but I must go now. Good-bye, mother! I
hope your painter will make himself very
agreeable." And the next moment Lord
Seaforth was gone.

Lady Seaforth felt very angry. She had hoped
—she had schemed—for her son's marriage
with Mrs. Trelawn, and here the reckless young
man was throwing his best chances away.
And for what motive? Could he have any
reason for not wishing to meet Mr. Vyner?
thought Lady Seaforth, as she extended her
hand and smiled a welcome to the painter.

Sitting at the head of her well-appointed
table, she was still thinking of her son. Care-
burdened was this proud lady with the heaviest
of cares, but her culture made her perfectly
able to conceal this. Only once she alluded to
Seaforth.

"I am so sorry," she said, addressing Vyner,

"that my son is not able to meet you to-day ; but he is on duty with his regiment. You know him, do you not ?"

"I know Lord Seaforth very slightly," answered Vyner, with a certain reserve of tone and manner that both Lady Seaforth and Nora noticed.

"He knows something about him," thought Lady Seaforth. "Can he have heard any foolish report about me and this wild young lord ?" thought Nora softly ; and both ladies glanced at the painter's face, who was standing with his eyes cast down.

But Lord Seaforth's name was never again mentioned during the evening. The graceful, well-bred hostess exerted herself to charm, and Vyner's presence made Nora look so much like the Nora of old that both Lady Seaforth and the painter regarded her with involuntary admiration.

"When she is looking so handsome, and Seaforth not to see her !" inwardly sighed Lady Seaforth.

"She is the sweetest woman upon earth," thought the painter, also with a sigh ; and when Nora rose to leave, he asked permission to escort her next door to her own house.

Nora smiled her answer. She put her little black-gloved hand timidly on the painter's arm as they left Lady Seaforth's portico together, and her touch for the moment made Vyner forget his betrothed.

"It is a fine night," he said. "Let us walk round the Square together, as we used to walk long ago."

"But—but we were in the country then," answered Nora, smiling, and glancing up softly at the painter.

"Let us imagine we are in the country now, then," said Vyner. "Let us be free for five minutes from all the conventionalities—ah, Nora—pardon me, I should say Mrs. Trelawn— why is the world so full of regulation codes and rules?"

Nora laughed—almost a merry laugh.

"I think, if I remember rightly," she said, "a certain Mr. Vyner in former days was not greatly given to follow either regulations, codes, or rules; but, perhaps he is changed now."

"No, he is not changed—not changed in everything, at least "

His voice trembled a little as he said the last

few words, for he was thinking he was not
changed to *her*, and the man's thought seemed
to vibrate through the woman's heart.

"It seems but yesterday," went on Vyner,
"but yesterday, Nora, when we used to meet
at Warbrooke. But it is a long yesterday,"
he added, with a sudden change of voice and
manner—the memory of Margaret Blythe had
tapped him on the shoulder—"and many
things have happened since then."

"Yes, many things," said Nora; "but one
thing has not changed—we—we are friends
still."

For a moment or two Vyner did not speak.
Words of love and tenderness were rising
unbidden to his lips. But he put the curb on,
and tried to think of Margaret, though his
trembling hand stole out and sought for
Nora's.

"We—we will not change," faltered Nora.

"There are linked souls, I think," said
Vyner, the passionate ring in his voice
betraying his heart; "and, go where we will,
do what we will, these invisible chains will not
break. But—but what folly I am talking," he
added. "What will you think of me, Mrs.

Trelawn—a middle-aged man—talking senti-
mental trash like a boy? But you must forgive
me—the old memories are to blame—the old,
old days——"

"They were happy days," said Nora,
tremulously.

"Yes," answered Vyner, abruptly, "too
happy—but we must not talk of them."

Nora felt hurt by the painter's words. She
looked up in his face when they were standing
a few minutes later at her own door, and was
struck with his expression. He was biting his
lips, and there was a frown on his brow, and
Nora sighed uneasily as she entered the grand
home which John Trelawn's love and wealth
had made her own.

CHAPTER IX.

NELLIE'S LOVERS.

THERE is no doubt that it is a pleasant thing to be self-satisfied. The man who has a good opinion of himself goes through the world looking blandly in a becoming mirror. A certain young Mr. James Saunders, who lived in the same street as the Blythes, was one of those happy personages. In mentally contemplating himself, he saw only his good qualities. He enumerated them thus :—"I am young, I am good-looking, I am well off—any girl would have me."

It will be seen by this that, among his other attractions, he was a bachelor. His father—Mr. James Saunders also—had been (what he termed) a medical practitioner, and he had continued a medical practitioner until he finally retired from all earthly avocations. A safe man this old-fashioned doctor had been considered by all the matrons in his neighbourhood, and to be considered a safe man pays. At all events, his reputation had paid Mr. James Saunders. He died in the goodly position of having a large balance at his bankers, landlord of many houses, and owner of sundry railway shares and other properties, which brought him in an excellent income ; and left this wealth firstly to his wife, and then to his only son.

Young James Saunders was sixteen when his father died, and for the next seven or eight years his mother did her best to make him unendurable. That is, she (morally) knelt down and worshipped him, and made a fool of him, until the lad fancied himself to be a totally different person to what he was.

He really was an ordinary-looking young fellow, with a pert expression and a pert tongue. He fancied himself to be witty, good-looking, and irresistible. The women (to use his own phraseology) had something to do with the latter delusion. Mr. James Saunders was heir to, and virtually in possession of twenty thousand pounds, and among the ladies with whom he associated this sum was magnified

into double the amount, and no doubt cast a
halo round Mr. James's common, somewhat
comic face. At some fancy ball he appeared
as "Puck," and among his facetious young
friends he was generally termed "Puck," being
pleased to be considered a "shrewd and
knavish sprite;" and he was also considered
very good-natured.

He was good-natured, if good-nature means
paying for any amount of brandy-and-soda's,
and for gloves and other small luxuries. But
he knew where to stop. Stories about him—
stories not pleasant to hear or to write about—
reached his adoring mother's ears, and the poor
woman was so shocked that she retired to bed,
and lay there weeping in bitter distress. Then
James promised to reform. He would be called
"Puck" no longer; he would give up dubious
acquaintances, and he would marry some lucky
girl, and make her a good husband.

It was at this period of his life that the re-
forming "Puck" enumerated his advantages,
and decided that no girl would refuse him.

"And I'll have the prettiest girl about here,"
he told his mother. "I'll have Nellie Blythe."

Mrs. Saunders made no objection to his

choice. The Blythes were respectable people ; Miss Blythe was an exemplary young woman, and Nellie was a very pretty girl, against whom Mrs. Saunders had never heard a word.

"Your dear father," she told James, "attended the Major when he first settled here, and always spoke of him with respect. Miss Blythe, too, is an excellent girl, and has been just like a mother to Nellie—and I am sure, my darling, I hope you will be happy !" And the fond mother clasped her son in her stout arms, and left a tear on his somewhat motley check.

She also never doubted that Nellie Blythe would be but too glad to marry her son.

"I'll write a note and ask them to dine with us in a friendly way on Thursday," she suggested to James, bent upon forwarding his matrimonial intentions; "and you can take the note yourself, my dear, and say how pleased we shall be to see them all, and tell them I'll take no refusal from the Major."

She was a very homely woman this, and had been a good wife to the late old-fashioned doctor, and lived in the heart of London pretty much as she had done in the country town from which the doctor had brought her. It had been a surprise to her to find herself left so well off when the doctor died, but the money did not console her for the loss of her husband.

"I have nothing now but James," she sighed, amid her tears, after they had carried away her dead; and as years passed on "James" continued to be the sole delight and pleasure of her life.

James was fond of the "old lady" (as he called her) in his way. She was "a decent old woman," he sometimes told his companions; and as we have seen, he promised to amend his life when he saw that he was giving real pain to his mother.

The idea of his marriage, therefore, was delightful to Mrs. Saunders, and she absolutely shed tears of joy after James had started on his proposed visit to Major Blythe's family.

Let us now follow James—James in a pink necktie and lavender gloves—decorated for the occasion to the best of his taste and ability. His round eyes looked a little rounder than usual when he rang at the Major's door, for though he was quite at his ease with some sort of women, he—in spite of his self-satisfaction

—felt a little shy at the prospect before him.

"But they'll jump at me," he reflected, screwing up his courage; and so he rang the Major's bell, prepared to be jumped at.

His summons was answered by the one maid-servant, Hatton, who of course knew James Saunders by sight, as Mrs. Saunders's house was close to the Blythes.

"Ladies at home?" asked James, jauntily.

Oblique-eyed Hatton put her hand contemplatively on her hip before she replied.

"They told me to say they're out," she said.

James hesitated a moment, and then slipped half-a-crown into Hatton's long, lean fingers.

"Tell them I've called," he said. "I've a message from my mother." And Hatton, being unable to resist the half-crown, James was ushered in on the two sisters.

Margaret was sitting before her easel, dressed in a plain dress, but looking a picture of neatness; Nellie was sitting on the floor, her fair, bright hair ruffled, engaged in forcibly washing the collar of white fur round Wallace's neck, decidedly against the old dog's desire.

Margaret rose gracefully as James entered the room, and held out her hand to welcome

him, though she darted a sharp look of anger
at Hatton, who received it unmoved, inwardly
fortified by the half-crown.

"You must excuse my sister, Mr. Saunders,"
said Margaret, glancing at Nellie, who had
jumped up, and was laughing, "but you see
she is washing our dog—he is such an old
favourite—especially of my father's."

Margaret always threw the best and most
attractive light that she could upon everything.
Yet she lacked the subtle gift which is usually
called tact. Her discernment was not acute
enough to possess this, and her intense egotism
displayed the want. Tact would have taught
her that nothing is so tiresome and offensive to
others as a self-adoring attitude, and this
Margaret habitually took. But as far as her wit
went, she put the most attractive and correct
colour upon all her own actions and those
of every one connected with her.

She was annoyed that Nellie should have
been caught washing the dog, but she need not
have been. James, indeed, was fond of dogs,
and had a bull-dog of his own, with a self-
important strut like his master's.

"Very kind of Miss Nellie," he said, looking

admiringly at Nellie standing there smiling, fresh and fair. "I like girls who like dogs; it shows some sort of—ah—you know what I mean."

"Sensibility," said Margaret, with her formal smile, as poor James paused for lack of ideas.

"Yes, kind heart, and that sort of thing. But,—ah!—Miss Blythe, I've called with a message from my mother. Hopes you'll all dine with us on Thursday. Won't excuse the Major. Mother said she would take no excuse."

"It is very kind of Mrs. Saunders," said Margaret. "I will ask my father." Margaret left the room for this purpose, and James was alone with the lady whom he proposed to honour with his hand.

Poor young man! This forward, pert youth, suddenly found that he had not a word to say. Nellie (who regarded him as "little Puck," this cognomen being well-known in the neighbour-hood) was, however, quite at her ease. She considered for a moment what she should say to him, and then said, smilingly—

"Have you been at any balls lately, Mr. Saunders?"

"One or two," answered James, trying to

seem at ease; "but don't care for 'em—
ordinary lot, I mean. Fancy balls are splendid,
Miss Nellie. Once went to one dressed as
'Puck'—fairy fellow, you know, out of Shak-
speare—glorious get up—all the fellows said
suited me—fond of fun, you know, and that
kind of thing."

"Yes," said Nellie, wickedly, "I've heard
you are fond of fun."

"Puck" blushed all over his motley skin.

" Mean to turn over a new leaf, Miss Nellie,'
he jerked out. "All very fine when one's just
out, you know, as you girls say; but when a
fellow gets on a bit—well, it's time to pull up."

"Yes," said Nelly, very much amused.

"Mother doesn't like it, you know," continued
" Puck," confidentially; " and she's a good old
woman that; and a fellow doesn't care to vex
her. Mean to settle down now, and become a
respectable jog-trot. Wild days are over, Miss
Nellie."

" Then we must not call you ' Puck ' any
more ?" said Nellie, with a little laugh.

" *You* may call me anything," said " Puck,"
tenderly; "anything nice, of course. I mean
—anything—"

At this moment the room door opened, and Margaret Blythe entered, and "Puck's" speech was interrupted.

"My father desires me to give his compliments to Mrs. Saunders," said Margaret, "and he and I shall be very happy to dine with her on Thursday, but you must kindly excuse Nellie."

"Can't, Miss Blythe; can't, indeed!" said James, energetically. "Miss Nellie must come —particularly want Miss Nellie."

"Very kind of you," said Nellie, "but I never go out to dinner."

"Oh, but do come," urged James. "Mother would be awfully sorry if you didn't—it would be so jolly to have you—must come, Miss Nellie."

"No, thank you," said Nellie, whose thoughts had wandered away from "Puck"— had wandered to Murray, Lord Seaforth, and was wondering if she could manage to meet him while Margaret and her father were dining with Mrs. Saunders.

Therefore, poor James urged his invitation in vain. Nellie was quite firm; and, much crest fallen, James at last took his departure, and returned to his mother's house in a very uncomfortable condition of mind.

That fond parent, however, did her best to console him.

"Girls of Nellie's age," she told him, "seldom go out to dine—and you know, my darling," she added, "she did not know your intentions."

"No," said James, brightening, "of course she didn't! If she'd known I meant *business*, I bet you anything she'd come."

"And you *really* do mean something serious, James?" asked Mrs. Saunders, looking lovingly at her son.

"I do," said James, solemnly. "It's a sacrifice, I know—a fellow has to give up a lot of things when he marries—and women are bothers with their great boxes to drag after one on every occasion—still "—and " Puck " sighed —" if one has to do it once in one's life, I want Nellie Blythe. She's awfully pretty, and awfully jolly, and though Margaret's a poser, and the old Major a bit of a bore, still I'll do it—you may tell her to-morrow, mother, that I'll do it, if you like; and I mean what I say."

Armed with this manly resolution on the

part of James, Mrs. Saunders actually did call the next day at the Blythes', and had an interview with Margaret.

Margaret could not understand what she was aiming at when she kept urging Nellie to dine with them.

"You see, my dear," she said, "I am most anxious James should settle. A better boy does not live—he's sweet-tempered like his dear father, and straightforward and full of pleasantry—but there it is—he's too high-spirited, in fact, and wants a wife to sober him down a bit—and I'm sure you'll persuade Miss Nellie to come on Thursday."

"I really do not know what to say, Mrs. Saunders," said Margaret. "It's really very kind of you, but——"

"James will be well off, too," continued the anxious mother; "very well off. His dear father left over twenty thousand, and, of course, it's all James's; and this last year my poor brother has gone to a better land, too, and I've come in for seven hundred a-year more, and I've made my will, and James has every penny of it!"

"He is a very fortunate young man," answered

Margaret, very gravely, for she now thought she began to perceive the drift of Mrs. Saunders's words.

"And his wife will be a fortunate young woman, I hope," said Mrs. Saunders, with rather a forced little laugh. "In fact, my dear, I may as well tell you what I'm driving at—James has taken a fancy to Miss Nellie, and I'll be delighted to have it settled; and so I hope you'll all come to dine on Thursday, and we can talk it over."

Margaret hesitated for a moment. She was considering the advantages of this proposal, and in her eyes they were great. The Blythes were in truth very poor—so poor that James Saunders's prospects seemed actually wealth. He was good-natured and he was young, thought Margaret, and both these latter qualities would suit Nellie.

"It is most kind and flattering of you, Mrs. Saunders," began Margaret. "Of course I can say nothing—but——"

"You're so much older than Miss Nellie that naturally your advice will have great influence on her," continued Mrs. Saunders; but our paragon's brow clouded at this allusion to her age.

"I'm not so much older, Mrs. Saunders," she said.

"Oh, no, my dear, I know you are quite young," quickly replied kindly Mrs. Saunders, vexed with herself for having made such a mistake, "but what I mean is, you're so clever and all that; your sister is sure to think a great deal of your opinion."

"I have always tried to do my duty, Mrs. Saunders," said Margaret, with conscious merit.

"You always have done it, you mean, my dear. My poor man, who is gone now, always admired you. He used to say there were few like Miss Margaret, and I feel sure if he were alive to do it, he'd give James, and Miss Nellie too, his blessing if they make a match of it."

"Then am I authorised to speak to my sister on this subject?"

"Of course, dear. James said he meant it. And, now I think of it, they're not unlike. Both have such pretty round little features— not quite regular, perhaps—but so full of expression and fun. I call Miss Nellie's a sweet face, and so I am sure is my James's."

Oh, fair Nellie Blythe! fair Nellie Blythe! She was not a vain girl this—glorying very

little in her gifts of youth and beauty—but to
be called like "little Puck!" Well was it for
Mrs. Saunders's matrimonial project that she
did not hear the comparison. As it was, Mrs.
Saunders returned to her James full of com-
placency.

"It's as good as settled, I consider, my
darling," she said to Puck ; and Puck's heart
sank a little at the news.

"It's like taking a header in the sea on a
March morning," he said, with an attempt at
facetiousness. But, all the same, he did not feel
very comfortable. Matrimony at a distance,
and matrimony so near, seemed very different
things to little Puck.

In the meantime the girl, whom he was
making so sure of marrying, was planning a
meeting with the man to whom she had given
her foolish, innocent heart. Nellie was not in
the least like a London girl. She was too poor,
and had lived too much out of the world, to
know anything about it. Ambition troubled
her not ; and as for society, she knew little or
nothing of it. The Major's income was too
small to afford ball dresses, even if Nellie had
had any balls to go to. She had never been at

school—Margaret being quite able to educate her young sister—so she had no girl companions of her own age. Margaret's friends were chiefly art students or governesses, and the Major's his ancient companions-in-arms, whom Nellie naturally regarded as old men. As for young men, she scarcely knew any. Little Puck, a medical student or two, sons of their immediate neighbours, were all the acquaintances Nellie could count until she met Lord Seaforth.

Here was a young man whom the instructed daughters of his class probably merely regarded as good-looking, cynical, and fast. But the uninstructed Nellie—comparing him with little Puck and the medical students—saw a man high-bred and graceful, and worthy of all her foolish, innocent love.

And Lord Seaforth. Never had this young lord paused in his career of pleasure from motives of prudence. He had paused from weariness; and, looking sadly and sourly back over the past few years of his life, he freely admitted to himself and others that at the best he had but played the fool.

But was he wiser now? A fresh and blooming face had struck his fancy: and thoughtless and reckless as ever, he wanted this fresh and blooming face for his own. Nellie was so sweet and fair, a young man might well be forgiven for committing some folly for her sake ; but Lord Seaforth knew all the while he went to meet Nellie Blythe that the folly of marrying her was an impossible one for him.

Yet still he went to meet her. It was the old symbol of the moth and the flame. Sweet Nellie Blythe was a very innocent flame, but no less surely the luring light might prove fatal in the end. But of this the young lord never thought. He thought of the lovely colour that bloomed and deepened through Nellie's smooth round cheeks, and he thought it was pleasant that this young creature should love him. In her pure love some of his lost youth seemed to return. "I cannot part with Nellie," he sometimes told himself, and sometimes the ruin that stared him in the face told him that he must.

Nellie was writing to this young man when Margaret, full of Mrs. Saunders' matrimonial ideas, sought her after Mrs. Saunders had left.

"Nellie," began the elder sister, "I have just had a visit from Mrs. Saunders."

"Hatton told me she was here," answered Nellie, looking up from her letter with a smile. " Well, had the old lady any news ? "

" She has been telling me about her son's prospects," said Margaret. " Had you any idea, Nellie, that young Mr. Saunders will be, nay, is now, very rich ? His father left him over twenty thousand pounds, and lately his mother has had seven hundred a year left her, and young James is to get it all."

" Lucky little Puck," said Nellie.

" Nellie, dear, I wish you wouldn't use those foolish nick-names. I do not like to hear them—they are not lady-like, and to a person of young Mr. Saunders's prospects they are certainly not appropriate."

Nellie laughed.

" Young Mr. James Saunders has my hearty congratulations, then, Margaret. Is that a proper way of putting it ? " she said.

" I want you to be in earnest, dear," said Margaret. " In fact, Nellie, I have a motive for telling you about Mr. James's prospects, and so had his mother. She wishes him to settle in life—she thinks a wife would sober him—"

"I've heard he wants a little sobering," laughed Nellie.

"There is nothing against him," said Margaret. "He has been a good son, and to be a good son or daughter means to be a good husband or wife. I judge by myself—I have tried, as you know, to be a good daughter, and I have no doubt that I shall make a good wife."

"Mr. Vyner will be the gainer, then, Margaret," said Nellie, looking very kindly at her sister.

"Yes, I think—I am sure, I shall make Walter happy. But I want you to be happy also, dear—and I think, as Mr. James is so well off, and so good-natured—"

Then Nellie looked straight up in her sister's face with a loyal light shining in her eyes.

"You are not in earnest about this, surely, Margaret?" she said. "You don't really mean that you want me to think of marrying little Puck?"

"Why not, Nellie? Mrs. Saunders wishes it, and Mr. James Saunders wishes it."

"Do not speak of such a thing any more, Margaret," said Nellie, earnestly—and she laid

her hand softly on the letter she was writing
—"for it can never, never be."

"I cannot see why, Nellie?"

"That is easily answered—because I do not
care for him—because I can never care for him."

"Girls change about these things."

"I will not"—and again the loyal light shone
in the blue eyes—"I will never change!"

She was thinking of Lord Seaforth—Lord
Seaforth, who was sitting at that moment
in Nora Trelawn's gorgeously - furnished
drawing-room, looking at Nora with his weary
eyes, and wondering with his weary heart if
he could sufficiently forget Nellie to make up
his mind to ask Crœsus's widow to be his wife.

But he did not make up his mind. Looking
at Nora, he still saw Nellie Blythe's sweet, fresh
face. He was not loyal to his love—he was
never loyal. He lacked the simple faith, the
fidelity of a larger mind. Yet he was in love
with the girl; in love, as he could love; and so
he did not progress in his wooing of Nora.

Still he sometimes went and talked to the
dark-eyed widow, and Lady Stainbrooke gave
him every encouragement to do so. This lady
had decided, from the time that she had heard

that the breath of life had quitted John
Trelawn's big body, that her niece, Nora, was
sure to marry again, and therefore she naturally
wished that she might marry well. To marry
well according to Lady Stainbrooke's ideas
meant to marry for certain worldly advantages.
Nora had wealth, so she now wanted rank,
thought her ladyship and her ladyship therefore smiled on, and ogled the young lord who
lived next door, as she had smiled and ogled in
the days when her own eyes were bright, and
when her heart was not perhaps so worldly as
it was now.

The young lord rather liked the worldly old
woman, for she helped to amuse him ; but Lady
Stainbrooke's company was gaul and wormwood
to his proud mother.

"You need never see her—afterwards—you
know," she once said to her son.

"Not my dear, dingy old aunt ! Mother,
how heartless you are. I shall, I assure you,
pay her the most tender attention."

"If you would but be in earnest, Seaforth,"
urged his mother.

"About Lady Stainbrooke ?" laughed the
young lord.

With an impatient gesture Lady Seaforth turned away. Yet that boyish laugh rang in her ears. It recalled his bright youth—the gay and gallant boy for whom she had hoped so much—hopes that one by one had faded and died away.

CHAPTER X.

ROSELAND.

ANOTHER man also came occasionally and sat
in Nora's gorgeously-furnished drawing-room,
on whom Lady Stainbrooke did not smile so
sweetly as she did on the spendthrift young
lord.

This was Vyner. Here again was the moth
and the flame. In this case the moth was
strong and clear-eyed. He knew the flame
was dangerous, but he depended upon his
strength. "I will go so far and no further.
I did love this gentle woman, and I do love her,
but I am bound in honour to another. Still, I
cannot quite forget my friendship for Nora—
cannot forget that but for a wicked old woman
Nora would now have been my happy wife."

Thinking thus, Vyner went occasionally to
see Nora. She was his friend—had been his

friend in the old happy days—and he was not going to turn coldly away. So he hovered near the flame, strong and clear-eyed. "There is no danger if I do not go too near," said the moth; "and why should I not gladden my sight occasionally by a gleam of sweet, pure light?"

Poor moth, poor flame! It is well to be strong and clear-eyed, but safer to go away into darkness. The world seemed very dark and weary now to Vyner unless he saw Nora, and so he did see her, and Lady Stainbrooke's blinking brown eyes sometimes showed their disapproval of his visits.

But Lady Stainbrooke was too much a woman of the world to be uncourteous to Vyner. He was a famous man, for one thing; for another thing it was Nora's house, and not Lady Stainbrooke's; and the old woman knew this as well as anyone else did.

One close evening in the middle of July, then, Vyner was sitting in Nora's drawing-room. There were also present General Stainbrooke and his wife, and Nora.

The old General was but a wreck now. There were days, nay weeks, when he was never seen

in the drawing-room, when he retired; and
during these days and weeks he did not see
much of Lady Stainbrooke.

But Nora was always very good to him.
She pitied him, racked with his sore pains, and
drifting away from his little tinsel-gilt life.
Poor man! he had even survived his age. He
belonged to a school that had grown too fusty
for the world—that had passed away, leaving,
it is to be hoped, newer and purer academies
behind it.

"And where do you think the General and I
are going to-morrow, Mr. Vyner," said Nora,
looking smilingly at the painter, a pause
having occurred a moment before in the
conversation.

"How can I tell! Well, where?" said Vyner.

"To Roseland?" answered Nora, still
smiling. "Is not that a pretty name?"

"Roseland!" repeated Vyner. "And where
is Roseland? And are you going to Roseland,
General?" he shouted to the old soldier.

The General emitted his cackling laugh, and
showed all his great yellow teeth.

"Where she goes I follow," he said.
"Always my way, Mr. Vyner—if a pretty

woman went before me I was after her—always my way."

" A very shocking way," laughed Vyner. " But where, Mrs. Trelawn, really, is Roseland ?"

Nora cast down her eyes, and a soft colour stole over her face before she answered.

" When Mr. Trelawn—when my husband was alive, Mr. Vyner," she said, " we had a little river yacht—"

" You had everything, my dear," said Lady Stainbrooke, with a little nod of her head at Vyner, pleased to give him a slight passing scratch.

" He was very good to me," continued Nora, still with her eyes cast down ; " and, as I was saying, we had a yacht ; and one day on the river, such a charming scent of roses came floating towards us that I asked Mr. Trelawn to stop the yacht, and we landed to try to get some roses if we could. Close to where we landed, a pretty little house in a garden, which sloped to the river edge, caught our attention, and John and I—Mr. Trelawn and myself— stood looking over the gate, and inside there was absolutely a rose show. I never saw such beautiful roses. And whilst we were standing looking, a young lady appeared in the garden, and passed close to the gate. 'We are admiring your roses,' my husband said to her, and she stopped and looked at us with a very wintry smile. 'Yes, they are pretty,' she said, and she shrugged her shoulders. 'They are beautiful!' answered my husband. 'I suppose we could not buy some of them?' 'No, they are not for sale; but I will give you some,' said the young lady. 'Will you come in?'"

"This is quite a romance," said Vyner, smiling, as Nora paused in her story.

"A very prosaic romance, as it turned out," answered Nora, smiling also. "But to go on with my romance. The young lady not only cut us the most lovely bunch of roses in the world, but she told us her little history. She had married an old and eccentric man for a home, and the old and eccentric man's chief passion was roses. So the young lady—not unnaturally, perhaps—was sick of roses. She told me their scent absolutely sometimes made her feel quite ill, and she was weary of her rose garden, and I fear also of her husband, and her home. John—Mr. Trelawn—was very fond of flowers, and before we parted with our young

lady he put his card in her hand. 'If ever you
can persuade your husband,' he said, 'to part
with this place, will you let me know?' and the
young lady promised to do so, and seemed very
pleased at the idea. But months passed away,
and we heard nothing from her. It was six
months afterwards, I think, when one day a
black-edged envelope came to John, and when
he opened it he found it was from the lady of
the roses, as we had christened her. Her
eccentric husband was dead, he had left her his
rose garden, and she would be glad to part
with it. Such were the contents of her letter,
and John was glad to buy it. It is a pretty
little place, and I asked leave to call it Roseland; and just now, when the roses are in their
bloom, it is quite lovely. John bought a little
land that joins it, and I have a cow there, and
I make butter, and I have eggs," laughed Nora;
"and, in fact, I am a farmeress in a small way
when I go to Roseland."

"And you like the country life? asked
Vyner.

"Far better than the town. My tastes are
really very simple," answered Nora.

"All very fine, my dear," said Lady Stain-

brooke; "very fine, and very pretty, to play
at simplicity sometimes among your roses,
when the sun is shining and the sky is blue.
But what about a real country life that your
young friend of the roses lived with her tiresome old man? She did not enjoy it, it seems.
No; solitude and sentiment are like poverty—
very well to have a peep at, and talk about, but
very bad to bear when they are forced upon us."

"You are not given to sentiment, Lady
Stainbrooke?" said Vyner, with a slight curl
of his lip.

"No," answered that lady briskly; "and the
consequence is, Mr. Vyner, that I have done
well for myself and my family, and that Nora
has now Roseland to go to, if she will excuse
me making the remark."

For a moment Nora looked annoyed, then
she said, very quietly—

"Well, at all events, Mr. Vyner, I hope you
will come and see Roseland?"

"I shall be but too happy," said Vyner. And
so it happened shortly after this, that, amid the
golden glory of a summer afternoon, Vyner
found himself walking by the river edge in
search of Roseland.

He never forgot the picture that he saw when he first entered Nora's garden. She was standing beneath her white sunshade, leaning on a little moss-grown wall, and gazing with a far-away look in her dark eyes at the river beyond.

She did not see him until he was quite close to her—until he almost touched her arm. The wearied look that he remembered on her face in her wedded days had passed away from it. Fair she had always been in Vyner's eyes, but never so fair as now, with the sweet pensive smile of hope lingering round her tremulous lips, as she stood in the sunlit garden.

Vyner did not speak. His eyes were fixed on the picturesque face and the picturesque form. But a slight movement that he unconsciously made attracted Nora's attention, and she looked round, and with a start recognised Vyner.

"You !" she said.

"Yes," he answered ; and then for a moment they stood hand-clasped, until, with womanly shyness, Nora turned away.

"I must show you my roses," she said, nervously.

"Yes," again answered Vyner, and he followed Nora all over her sweet-scented domain.

It was literally as she had told him, a rose garden. The rarest and most beautiful roses were here, and every species and variety ever reared by the hand of man. And the wild crimson hedge-rose was blooming among the rest. There were no other flowers, only the roses, and Vyner was charmed with the beauty of the effect.

"Amongst all this wealth," he said, "do you think you can afford to give me one?"

"Yes, or even a bunch," smiled Nora, in reply.

"I shall be content with one," he said; and Nora stooped down and gathered him a moss rosebud.

"I think you will like this," she said, "better than the grand ones."

Vyner did not answer. He took the rosebud, and the hand that held it. They were close to the moss-grown wall where Nora had been leaning when Vyner first entered the garden, and which separated the grounds of Roseland from the narrow pathway by the river edge.

A little moss-grown parapet of stone. The damps and mists from the river had stained it green, and the moss flourished on it, and the ivy crept round its time-worn basement. Here Vyner leaned with Nora, hand-clasped, the rosebud between the love-bound fingers.

All sunlight! The glory of the sun on the river and meadow lands, and the flowers—and Nora's heart, for did not the man she loved love her? she was whispering to herself; and so the glory and brightness of her life seemed full.

But suddenly Vyner dropped the hand and the rose; dropped the rose in forgetfulness, but the hand meaningly. He had remembered Margaret Blythe, and a cloud had arisen in the sky.

Nora looked surprised. She saw the rosebud fall, and she saw the cloud come over Vyner's face, and she wondered at the cause. Then, after a moment's reflection, she thought that she had guessed it.

"It is because I am rich," she thought. "Ah, Walter, how can you so misjudge my heart?"

"How is the General?" asked Vyner, abruptly, the next minute.

"I left him sitting reading the papers under the awning of the verandah," answered Nora. "Will you come and talk to him?"

The verandah ran along the whole of the front of the one-storied house. John Trelawn had built this verandah after he had bought Roseland, and it was therefore fitted up with every luxury that wealth could supply.

Sitting beneath the shade of its pink-and-white striped awnings, they found the General. The verandah itself was very pretty; roses were trained up its rustic pillars, and on a rustic table at the General's elbow a dish of splendid strawberries was standing. The old General was reading the newspaper with "spectacles on nose," as they approached him; but no sooner did he see them than he hastily removed these useful but unornamental instruments, and shuffled them into his coat pocket.

"Ah, Mr. Vyner," he said, with his grand air, holding out one of his lean and crippled hands, but not rising to welcome the painter, for indeed he could not. "So you have found us ruralising. A pretty spot; and my niece, Mrs. Trelawn, becomes her roses, eh? Sweets to the sweets, eh? That's about it! Ha, ha, ha!"

"Yes," said Vyner, turning round, and looking quietly at Nora with his grey, handsome eyes, "she becomes her roses."

Nora blushed like a girl.

"It's pleasant to get out of the world sometimes, eh, Mr. Vyner?" continued the old
soldier. "You painters, I suppose, get your
ideas—your—whatever d'ye call them?"

"Inspirations!" suggested Nora, in her
loudest tone, in the General's ear.

"Don't speak quite so loud, my love," said
the General, rubbing that organ with an injured
air. "Inspirations!—ah, ah, to be sure—so
you call your pictures inspirations, d'ye, Mr.
Vyner? Devilish bad inspirations, then, some
pictures are, that's all I can say. Ha, ha, ha!"

Vyner laughed heartily at this sally.

"Don't be so hard on us, General!" he
shouted.

"Bit of a judge, you know," said the General.
"Like a bit of colour—always did—and 'the
light that lies in woman's eyes'—that's my
taste still—can admire a pretty woman still,
painted or unpainted!"

Again Vyner laughed—this time grimly.

"But you painters—you modern men, I
mean—don't come up to my ideas of beauty,"
continued the General. "I like colour, flesh,
plumpness, &c."

"No woman can be beautiful in my eyes," said Vyner, "unless she has a beautiful mind —beauty to me is the semblance of the soul."

"Of the soul! What the deuce has the soul to do with it? You can't paint a soul?" said the General, testily, for he had not quite caught Vyner's words.

"But I can recognise it," said Vyner.

"I am a practical man," proceeded the General, "and a pretty face is composed of fine features, according to my ideas, and of a fine skin, and not of soul. But Nora, my love, won't Mr. Vyner taste your strawberries? They are very fine."

"You are a practical man to some purpose now," laughed Vyner, and he sat down by the General's table and ate some of his strawberries.

But by-and-by the General's head began to nod. He tried—ever gallant—to keep himself awake in the presence of a lady, but the worn-out old machine wanted rest, and rest it would have. Vyner's voice grew distant and dim in his ears, and Nora's unheard. He had fallen asleep, and presently announced this fact by loud and discordant snores.

Vyner and Nora looked at each other and smiled.

"Poor old man!" said Nora, softly.

"It's well to be old," said Vyner, in the bitterness of his heart—he still remembered Margaret. "Age deadens our feelings. Yes, it is well to be old."

CHAPTER XI.

MARGARET SETTLES IT.

WHILE Nora and Vyner were wandering together in the rose garden by the river, fate, in the shape of Margaret Blythe, was preparing to end such meetings.

Margaret was wonderfully self-reliant and self-satisfied. Still, a feeling of uneasiness of late had been creeping over Margaret's mind regarding Vyner's manner towards herself.

He had never been a very demonstrative lover. But he had been kinder, tenderer, surely, to her once? Again and again Margaret had thought this, and she had thought also, could there be any cause, and if so, that it were well to discover it.

Once or twice, when she had asked him to spend the evening with them, he had said he was engaged.

"And where are you going, Walter?" Margaret had asked.

"To Mrs. Trelawn's—she is an old friend of mine," Walter had answered; and Margaret began to ponder about this old friend, and by-and-by heard that she was rich, and that she was a widow—that she went by the name of "Crœsus's widow."

"You knew this lady long ago, then, Walter?" Margaret said one day, alluding to Nora.

"Yes," answered Vyner, very briefly.

"Before she was married?" asked Margaret.

"Yes," again answered Vyner, and then he began to talk quickly on some other subject.

But Margaret did not forget this conversation about Crœsus's widow. She remembered it, and determined to act upon it. She was motherless, but so self-reliant a young woman required no mother.

"Father," she said, addressing the blind Major a few days afterwards, her usual equal measured tones being a little disturbed, "don't you think that it is time that something was definitely settled about—my marriage?"

The Major lifted his bent head with a slightly surprised air.

"Well, my dear," he said, "of course, if you and Mr. Vyner wish it. It will be a great loss to me; but little Nellie and I must get on as best we can."

"Dear father," said Margaret—for she really was a good daughter—"I would not be happy if I were to leave you. No; I have a different scheme to propose. Nellie is a dear little girl, but she is scarcely competent to take charge of a household, I think. What I wish is this— that you will live with myself and Walter, and that Nellie will marry young Mr. Saunders and live in the house with the old lady."

"What, little Puck!" exclaimed the Major. "Why, Margaret, what an idea!"

"Father, it is a very good idea. But I wish you would not call James Saunders 'little Puck,' just as Nellie does. Do you know how well off he is, father? Mrs. Saunders herself told me a day or two before we dined there last that the old doctor left James over twenty thousand pounds, and Mrs. Saunders has lately been left seven hundred a year by her brother, and this also goes to James."

The blind Major sighed. Want of money had been one of the burdens that he had been called upon to bear all his life. He had married for love, and it had been all that he could do to pay his way and pass as an honest man among his fellows. He was very poor, and small luxuries and even comforts were unknown in the economical household managed by Margaret's careful hand.

James Saunders's prospects, therefore, seemed to open a vista of wealth to the poverty-stricken Major. He was a good, simple man this— simple and God-fearing—but he was not a man of keen perceptions. His sightless eyes, of course, had never beheld the common, comic face of "little Puck." He might be a good fellow enough, thought the Major, but Nellie was his darling.

"He may be rich," he said; "but Margaret, my dear, unless Nellie likes him, I could not urge her to think of him—besides, do you know that the young man wishes this?"

"His mother formally proposed for him," answered Margaret. "I told her Nellie had never thought of young Mr. James; that we were not girls to think of young men until we were asked to do so; but I advised her to tell Mr. James to come here sometimes, and I feel sure Nellie, who knows now from me that he seriously admires her, will think of him—could very easily learn to care for him, if she chose."

"But she may not choose."

"Father, you know how annoyed I was about Lord Seaforth. I have since learned from Walter that this young lord bears a terrible character. Among fast men he is one of the fastest, and at one time I feared—I wish to be quite honest with you—that Nellie liked him too well for her own happiness."

"I pray God not—my poor, innocent darling," murmured the Major.

"This is one reason I am so anxious she should marry," continued Margaret. "As for marrying Lord Seaforth, that of course is out of the question. His rank would prevent it for one thing, and for another I am told he is absolutely overwhelmed with debt. The sooner, therefore, that Nellie forgets him the better."

"Yes, indeed," said the Major.

"And James Saunders is young and rich, and very good-natured," urged Margaret, "and is really fond of Nellie. Mrs. Saunders says he is very fond, and he will settle money on her, and altogether it is a good match. Now, don't you think so, father?"

"Yes, if the little one likes him."

"Oh, girls like Nellie easily like and dislike. You persuade her to think of him, father. And now about something else—about Walter?"

"Well, dear?"

"Walter is very well off now—he gets great prices for his pictures, and he must be saving money very fast, for he does not spend much. And I do not see why we should not be married at once. In fact, dear father, I want you to speak to him. It is so wearing to a girl to have a long engagement, and I think it should be settled."

The Major was silent. He was a gentleman, and he felt that the task his daughter proposed for him was anything but a pleasant one.

"It would be so nice if it were all settled," continued Margaret. "Walter can quite afford to take a good house, and you could live with us, and I am sure we would be all very happy together—for I have the gift, I think, of retaining affection."

"But, my dear," said the Major, "I could not possibly propose to Mr. Vyner to live with you. Of course, as you say, it is very wearing to a woman, a long engagement, and I can ask him to settle it; but as for proposing to live with him myself, it is out of the question."

"But, father, Walter is just a man to honour filial affection. He knows your affliction binds you closer to me. I am sure he would not wish us to part, and I am sure also that I can make you both very happy."

"My dear Margaret, any offer of this kind must come from Vyner. I will speak to him, if you wish, about your marriage; but I will certainly not speak to him about anything else."

"Well, dear father, as you please. If you will kindly speak to him about making arrangements for our marriage, I dare say I shall be able to manage the rest, for I have a great deal of influence on Walter."

Up the river in the rose garden, on the very day when this conversation took place, Walter was standing hand-in-hand with Nora Trelawn. Up the river in the rose garden the painter, with fast-beating pulses and a heart stirred to its very depths, was leaning on the little stone-work parapet, close, very close, to sweet Nora Trelawn. Nora in her soft womanly prime, with the sunlight in her eyes and in her heart!

But the painter was to pay a very bitter price for his brief forgetfulness. When he returned in the evening from Roseland he found a note lying on his table at home from his betrothed Margaret. It was to invite him to call on the following evening, "as my father has a few words to say to you, dear Walter," wrote Margaret; and Vyner felt that he could scarcely refuse to go.

So about eight o'clock he found himself ringing at the Major's door-bell. Hatton, her quaint face shining with soap for the occasion, opened the door, grinning her welcome.

"Tea's in, sir," she said, "and they're waiting for ye;" and then she opened the little sitting-room door.

In the room Vyner found the two sisters, "Little Puck," and the blind Major. "Little Puck" was describing a piece he had seen acted the night before. Some little humour had "Puck," and the facetious contortions of his face were making Nellie laugh in spite of herself. "Puck" felt that he was successful; and, as he afterwards declared to his fond parent, "a wet blanket seemed to be thrown over the whole party when Vyner walked in."

There was some truth in this. Vyner himself, with care on his handsome face, certainly did not look in a humour to add to any conviviality. Margaret was anxious and the Major uncomfortable. And Nellie? Ah, Nellie, there was care in your heart also—care and great anxiety, and a secret too—for on the morrow she had promised to meet Lord Seaforth, and give him an answer to a question which he had asked before.

But Margaret was always composed in manner, whatever were her secret anxieties. She rose and received Vyner with a smile, poured out some tea for him, and talked to him about the weather and his pictures.

"And have you finished the painting you call 'Eve?'" asked Margaret.

"No; I have turned its face to the wall," answered Vyner.

"It certainly was not my conception of 'Eve,'" replied Margaret's even tones. "What do you think, father? Should she be a bright, dark, certainly rather a pretty woman, like Walter had drawn her; or a lovely, soft, fair piece of perfection, as I always mentally pictured our first mother ?"

"I should say the soft fair piece of perfection," said the Major. "But I am no judge of art."

"Is your 'Eve' a fancy sketch or a portrait," asked Margaret. "I should say a portrait."

"I hardly know," answered Vyner.

"It must be good fun to be able to paint—pretty faces especially," said little Puck. "Once thought of being an artist myself—can sketch away little heads, you know, and all that lot ; but to be the regular thing—to go in for it, you know, requires heaps, piles of work, and I'm too—what dy'e call it, for that ?"

"Too volatile," suggested Vyner.

Little Puck laughed good-naturedly. He was, in truth, really good-natured. A vain little fellow, but, as his adoring mother had said, "he had a good heart."

Presently Margaret whispered a word in her father's ear, and the blind Major rose obediently, and, assisted by Margaret, groped his way out of the room, going to a small sitting-room at the back of the house, which Margaret called "My father's study."

"My father's study" was very dingy. The

outward signs and indications of poverty are like the grains of sea sand upon the shore. The poor little packets of groceries, the miserable little scrag-ends of meat, washed-out covers, darned, faded carpets, black horsehair, with the white seams of age and bareness appearing on the surface. All these signs were to be seen in the Major's household, and the dingiest and poorest-looking place of all was "my father's study."

Here in his everlasting darkness the blind Major mostly lived. Always in the night—and yet, who knows? Have the blind ever visions—glimpses perhaps, of things beyond, which we of earthly ken cannot see?

Margaret having carefully escorted her father to his room, went back to the front sitting-room and sat down for a moment or two by the side of her betrothed, Walter Vyner.

"Walter, dear," she said, "will you go into my father's study for a few moments, for he is anxious to speak to you about—something important?"

"Certainly," answered Vyner, and he rose and went into the Major's study.

Major Blythe was looking a little disturbed

as he entered. The task which Margaret had
prepared for him was not a pleasant one to a
man of delicate feelings. Still the Major felt
that if Margaret wished it, it was his duty to
speak to Vyner. Vyner, unsuspicious of what
was before him, addressed the Major in his
usual manner.

"Well, Major," he said, "Margaret tells me
you want to speak to me."

"Yes, a few words," answered the Major,
nervously. "You see, my dear fellow, my—
my girls have no mother—"

Then Vyner knew what was coming.

"You lost your wife when they were very
young, did you not?" he said, nervously also.

"Yes, poor darling—she left me when little
Nell was almost a baby—but she has had a
mother in Margaret. Margaret is an excellent
girl, Vyner—a girl in a thousand."

"I am sure of that."

"But you see, girls who are engaged get
unsettled. In fact, my dear Vyner, Margaret
is unsettled—and—and I think it is time that
something was arranged about her marriage."

For a moment or two Vyner was silent.
For a moment or two a cold, dead, physical

pain crept into his heart, and with an effort he roused himself to answer.

" You mean," he said, " she wishes—"

" She wishes the time of her marriage to be fixed. It is only natural, you see, Vyner, and she asked me to speak to you ; and I am sure you will do everything in your power to please her."

" I will see about—arranging it," said Vyner, slowly. He did not blame Major Blythe. He knew he had no right as an honourable man to ask another man's daughter to marry him, and not be ready to fulfil that engagement. But this conversation came as a blow to him—a sudden, bitter blow.

But yesterday—but yesterday at Roseland ! And now that dream must be ended—ended as it had ended five long years ago, in bitter disappointment and pain.

" I will see Margaret," he said, struggling to speak calmly, "and—and I suppose we will settle it."

" Yes, do, my dear fellow ! and let me tell you, you are a lucky man. Margaret has been a pattern daughter, and she will make a pattern wife."

"The lucky man" laughed feebly, and then rose to leave the Major's study, and he hoped the house. But Margaret, who had been listening for his footstep, opened the front sitting-room door, as he was seeking for his hat in the little hall, and at once advanced towards him.

"You are not going, are you, Walter, surely?" she said.

"I have some work to do, Margaret," answered Vyner, "so I must be off at once."

"Has—has my father said anything to you?" asked Margaret, anxiously.

"Yes—and we will talk it over the next time I come. Good-night, Margaret." And Margaret held up her face to receive her lover's kiss.

"Good-night, dearest," she whispered. "You will come to-morrow, then—and we will settle it."

.   .   .   .

It was starlight when Vyner went out. In times of great mental darkness, do not the still heavens seem to mock our woe? There— serene, unmoved, star-diadem'd, while we stand passion-toss'd, impotent in our rage or grief.

Here was Vyner—a painter, a man who loved his work and God's work, and who had lived believing that yon blue luminous vault above but veils from us greater glories; yet here was Vyner looking upwards with a curse on his lips, and with his hands clenched, and with weariness, nay, rage in his heart, at all things on earth below.

Why had he hung this stone about his neck? he was asking himself. Why had he been permitted in his blindness to do so? He had never loved Margaret Blythe. He had respected and admired her for her meritorious endeavours to assist her family, and he had believed her to be a good woman, and seen that she liked him, and feeling unsettled, and not very happy, he had drifted into an engagement with her.

When he knew more of her, he saw how narrow and self-appreciative her mind was; he saw, in fact, that they were unsuited to each other; and shortly after he had come to this conclusion he met again the one woman that he had ever really loved. He learned that this one woman was a widow; and he learned also, when he looked in her dark eyes, that this one woman loved him still.

"Why, then," he asked, in the great bitterness of his soul, after his interview with Major Blythe, "had a wicked old woman been permitted to spoil two lives by a miserable lie?" But for this Nora might have been his happy wife, her children prattling by his knee.

So there was great darkness on the soul of Vyner. He felt that he was bound hand and foot, and he felt also that honour at once demanded a bitter sacrifice from him, which was to tell Nora of his engagement to Margaret Blythe.

"I will go to Roseland to-morrow," he told himself, wandering up and down with impatient strides in the terrace where he lived, beneath the starlight. "Yes, she shall know; and I would rather be dead than do what is now forced upon me."

CHAPTER XII.

HE went the next day to Roseland. He went in the evening, and to his great annoyance found "that wicked old woman," as he had mentally called Lady Stainbrooke so many times the night before, sitting admiring the sunset in the rose garden with her husband and Nora.

Lady Stainbrooke was in good humour, for she had just enjoyed a good dinner, and she held out her yellow claw-like hand, glittering with the diamonds she had contrived to pick up during her long sojourn in India, to welcome the painter as he approached them.

But Vyner did not take it. He shook hands with Nora and Sir Thomas, but bowed coldly enough to her ladyship, who, however, only gave a little laugh.

"What!" she said, "have I offended you?"

"We never were very good friends, Lady Stainbrooke," answered Vyner.

"No, no!" said Lady Stainbrooke, nodding her head. "All the same, in your inmost heart, I believe you must feel very much obliged to me." And again Lady Stainbrooke laughed, this time with rather a wicked ring in it, for she believed that Vyner came courting Nora for the money that John Trelawn had left behind.

Vyner quite understood her little insinuation. He stood there grim, pale, and handsome, looking at this "miserable old woman," as he was mentally designating her, and wishing her —well, the painter was angry, so we need not follow all his thoughts.

But Nora tried to be a peace-maker.

"Even Lady Stainbrooke is charmed with my roses, Mr. Vyner," she said smiling.

"Of course I am, my dear," said that lady. "I am charmed with your roses because they are pretty, and are cared for by a good gardener, for whom you can afford to pay. And I am charmed also with your cows, and your ducks and chickens, because they, too, have everything they require. But I would not be charmed with any of them if they were not merely a whim of a rich woman ; ruralising for amusement, and ruralising for life, are two very different things."

"Mr. Vyner has not seen my cows, nor my ducks and chickens, aunt, which you despise," said Nora. "Shall we show them to him now ?"

"I am very well where I am, my dear," answered her aunt drily.

"I should like of all things to see them," said Vyner eagerly.

"Come with me, then," said Nora. And as the painter followed her, Lady Stainbrooke rose and screamed her opinion into her deaf General's ear.

"My opinion is," she said, "that Nora will make a fool of herself and marry that man. It is a thousand pities, when Lord Seaforth would, I am sure, be only too glad to have her."

"What folly !" said the General, testily, in reply. "What makes you think, madam, she will take this painter fellow ?"

"Because," answered Lady Stainbrooke, grimly, "she is insane enough, I believe, to be in love."

The General grunted. This couple were not in love with each other—had not been in love for thirty years. They snarled at each other, and were very clear-eyed about each other's faults, but they went on living with each other —in all probability would so live until two of their bleared and worldly eyes were closed for evermore. That these would be the General's eyes Lady Stainbrooke was very happily persuaded. She frequently talked of "when I'm a widow," but the old man was in no hurry to place her in that position.

Meanwhile let us follow Nora and Vyner. Nora went bareheaded, with a rosy flush on her soft cheeks, and with her eyes cast down so that she never noticed how pale Vyner was, or how gloomy, as he walked by her side.

Nora's cows lived in a little field at one side of the rose garden, separated from it by a highly ornamental paling which was thickly trained with rose trees. A rustic gateway led through this paling to the field beyond, but as Nora laid her hand on the gate to open it Vyner prevented her.

"I do not really care about seeing your cows, Nora," he said, with rather a painful smile. "Will you put on your hat and walk down by the river with me? I—I—have something to say to you."

Nora looked up surprised. Then she saw how pale and agitated Vyner really was, and she at once did what he asked.

"Wait here for me a moment, then," she said; and she went into the house for her hat, while Vyner, leaning on the paling, was nerving himself for the bitter task before him.

He looked round when he heard her return, and then, without a word, the two together quitted the grounds of Roseland.

They went down by the darkening river, for the sun had set now, and dusky shadows had fallen on the water. Still in silence. Nora was nervous, and Vyner trying to frame his cruel news in gentle words. Then with sudden passion and abruptness he spoke, feeling that gentle words were vain.

"Nora," he said, "I have come to tell you something to-night that I would rather tear my tongue from my mouth than utter."

"What is it, Walter?" asked Nora, trembling.

"Let me go back," said Vyner, still in the

same agitated and passion-broken voice, "to the days long ago—to the days when you were a young girl, and—and I loved you then, Nora."

Nora did not speak. She put her hand softly on the painter's arm.

"I went back to Warbrooke," continued Vyner, "to ask you to be my wife. I was poor then—a man who had a struggle to live—but something in your face had told me that you were a good woman—that you would marry a man because you loved him, and not because he was rich."

"You know how it was," said Nora, in a low tone.

"I am coming to that. I went back to Warbrooke then, and found that you were gone. I was received coldly enough at your father's house, but I learned in the little town that you had gone to live with your father's sister, Lady Stainbrooke, in London, and that you were expected by your family to make a good marriage there."

"You did not believe *that*?"

"No, I did not. I told myself the little girl I love will do nothing of the kind—she will wait for me—wait till I can make a home for her."

Vyner's voice broke here, and Nora clasped his arm closer.

"Hush," she said, "do not talk of these painful things. They are all over now. My poor husband is dead now."

"Yes," said Vyner, bitterly, "and you are free! The cursed story that Lady Stainbrooke invented to part us was not true, as you know, then, Nora, but now—"

"There is no lie to part us now, Walter," said Nora firmly, "I am free and you are free—"

"No!" interrupted Vyner hoarsely. "That wicked, miserable old woman's work is not yet done. Nora, months and months ago—when you were Mr. Trelawn's wife—there crossed my path a woman—I believe a good woman—"

But Nora stopped him with a sudden cry.

"You are not married!" she said. "Walter, tell me" (and she clung with trembling hands to his arm), "surely you are not married?"

"No," he answered, averting his eyes from her frightened, appealing face; "not married— but bound by a promise that I cannot break."

Nora grew faint and cold.

"It cannot be," she said, still clinging to his arm. "Walter, it cannot be!"

"What can I say, Nora?" answered Vyner, clasping her cold and nerveless hand. "You know how it is—I cared for you long ago—I care for you now—but we are parted. In a moment of madness, I think—feeling sad, lonely, and dissatisfied with my lot, I asked Margaret Blythe to be my wife. She is a good woman—I have nothing to say against her—but when I saw you again I knew I had made a fatal mistake."

Nora could not now control the bitter emotion of her heart. Her eyes filled with tears, and she trembled so violently that Vyner asked her to sit down on the river bank.

It was a very lonely spot where they were, and as they sat down, with a sort of moan Nora covered her face with her hand.

"I have suffered so much," she said, "no one knows how much, in those long years— and now—now—"

There was a weary hopelessness in her tone, which touched Vyner to the quick.

"If I could do anything, Nora," he said, earnestly, "anything, anything, I would do it.

But Margaret Blythe is poor—I got to know her through a friend, who thought that perhaps in time she might become an illustrator of books, and so introduced her to me to see if I could push her on. This very fact—her poverty—makes it more difficult—"

"Still, perhaps, if she knew," said Nora, looking up, "knew that long ago we cared for each other so much, and that we were only parted by a wicked, wicked invention—"

Vyner was silent. He was a proud man— with a rough and honest pride in bearing a good name among his fellows—and he was thinking even if Margaret consented to their engagement being broken off, what would the world say? To throw over a poor girl for a very rich woman! Yes, he knew what it would say; for Nora's sake he would have borne much—but Margaret—

"You think it would be cruel to ask her," faltered Nora.

"I do not know what to say. Her father spoke to me the other night about fixing the time for our marriage. This determined me to tell you—I should never have come near you, Nora—never—but I was weak—"

They sat there together after this almost in silence. The great broad river kept rolling on before them, the twilight crept around them, but still they scarcely spoke. Nora felt miserably unhappy. She had loved Vyner so deeply, and all through the long years of her wedded life she had never forgotten him. The handsome face that had been the *beau-ideal* of her girlhood was her *beau-ideal* still. And now when she had dreamed—nay, been sure—of happiness, to have it all snatched away—all, and nothing left !

At last she rose.

"Are you going now ?" said Vyner, turning his head towards her ; and looking at him she saw how haggard his face was, how worn and grief-lined.

There was a great struggle in his heart. Honour or dishonour ! To forsake Margaret— dishonour ; to leave Nora—a long, weary, loveless life.

"Perhaps you will write ?" said Nora, in a low tone, as they walked on by the river edge towards Roseland.

"Yes," answered Vyner, speaking as with

an effort. "I will see Margaret—I will let you know what she says."

"You will tell her—the truth ?"

"Yes," again answered Vyner ; and without any further words on the subject of all-absorbing interest in both their hearts, they parted at the gate of Roseland.

As Nora walked through the garden a feeling of great and bitter anger rose in her heart against her aunt, Lady Stainbrooke.

"She has caused all this," she thought ; "all the misery of my life. I might have been a happy woman but for her false and lying tongue."

Full of her wrongs she entered the house. She could see, as she crossed under the verandah, her aunt sitting in the pretty luxurious drawing-room beyond. Lady Stainbrooke was lying back in an easy chair, with her feet very comfortably cushioned on a low chair before her, reading some very piquant novel, for Lady Stainbrooke loved properly-veiled immorality well. She was therefore thoroughly enjoying her novel, by the aid of the double glasses which before her family she now generally wore.

Then flushed, passionate, angry, Nora
entered the room, and Lady Stainbrooke
looked up and peered at her curiously through
her glasses.

"Well, my dear," she said, "and what have
you done with your painter?"

"You are a wicked woman, Aunt Stainbrooke!" answered Nora, to the great astonishment of that lady; "a bad, wicked woman, and
I wish I had never seen your face!"

Lady Stainbrooke put down her ugly little
feet, and removed her double glasses with a
jerk.

"You forget yourself, Nora, my dear," she
said; "utterly forget yourself."

"Not so utterly as you forgot yourself,"
retorted Nora, "when you invented that wicked
falsehood long ago about Mr. Vyner."

"Oh! that old story!" said Lady Stainbrooke, shrugging her shoulders. "Bah! my
dear, do not be so absurd. What do you
want? If you want this Vyner, he's ready to
go down on his knees to you—yes, a deal faster
than he went when you were a penniless girl."

"That is all you know," said Nora, standing
before her aunt, pale and trembling; "but you

believe in nothing good nor nothing true. You have spoilt my life!" And Nora having said this, turned and left the room.

Then Lady Stainbrooke rose and approached her General, who had not heard a single word that had passed between the two ladies.

"Did you hear what Nora said, General?" shouted Lady Stainbrooke in her husband's ear. "She has utterly forgotten herself—utterly forgotten what is due to me; and I shall leave the house at once, and you must come with me."

But Sir Thomas had no idea of turning out of such comfortable quarters on so short a notice.

"What do you say, madam?" he said. "Leave the house at once for some foolish women's quarrel? Not I. What on earth have you and Nora been rowing about?"

"I was not rowing," shouted Lady Stainbrooke, with an attempt at dignity. "Nora has forgotten herself. She has had some quarrel with this Vyner, and so she chose to attack me. But she may marry him. I give her up, after all I have done for her. I wash my hands of her, and I will order the carriage and return to town; and certainly you will not refuse to go with me?"

"But I certainly shall," answered the General, who was not going to expose his aching bones to the damp air by the river at this time of night. "I shall encourage no such folly. If you choose to go, *go*; but don't expect me to be such a fool as to go with you."

"You are contemptible!" hissed Lady Stainbrooke; and then in a towering rage she walked out of the room, and very shortly afterwards out of the house.

CHAPTER XIII.

NELLIE'S TEMPTATION.

MARGARET BLYTHE expected Vyner to call, on the night that his unhappy interview with Nora took place at Roseland, but he never came. She felt a little uneasy and nervous about this, but on reflection reassured herself.

"He has had some work to finish. I shall see him to-morrow," she decided in her calm way.

Then her eyes happened to fall on the fair face of her sister Nellie.

"Why, Nellie, how flushed you are!" said Margaret. "Has anything annoyed you?"

Nellie's blooming face turned a deeper pink at these words.

"No, Margaret dear," she said, and she went up and took her sister's hand.

"You are trembling, too," said the practical

Margaret. "I am afraid you are going to be ill. Do you think you have got a chill anywhere?"

"Oh, no," laughed Nellie, with an uneasy laugh, and Margaret, reassured on this point also, took up her housekeeper's book, and began to enter—as was her wont—every penny of their expenditure during the day.

But careful housekeeper as Margaret was, could she have looked into Nellie's heart, she would have neglected her accounts. During the day a very trying interview had occurred to Nellie—an interview which, had Margaret known of, she would have been really unhappy about her young sister.

When lowering clouds gather, we seldom escape a storm. Lowering clouds had been gathering long round the head of Murray, Viscount Seaforth, but the reckless young man made no effort to evade them. Nay, in his love, or his selfishness—he called it love—he had made up his somewhat unstable mind to endeavour to persuade Nellie to share his uncertain future. Yes, he loved her too dearly to give her up, he had decided during one of their recent interviews, and during their meeting this day—the day Vyner had told Nora of his engagement to Margaret—Lord Seaforth had urged Nellie to marry him secretly. "For to do it any other way," he told her, "would only bring irremediable ruin on us both."

"But I cannot—I cannot marry," the girl answered in tremulous accents, holding both his hands, "I cannot, for my father's sake."

"Then 'father' is more to you than I am?" said Lord Seaforth, half-tenderly, half-mockingly.

"He is blind," said Nellie, and her lips quivered.

"I wish I was blind!" said Lord Seaforth, with a little laugh.

"He would feel it so deeply," continued Nellie, pleadingly. "If I could but tell him, Murray—"

"And ruin me, my little girl?"

"I will never do that—never."

"Under no temptation, eh?"

"No, never," repeated Nellie. And the day was yet to come when he asked her to keep this promise.

They were standing together, these two

young people, under one of the great spreading trees in Regent's Park, when Nellie made it. Overhead the white-flecked summer sky, and around them the summer air, and the white butterflies on the wing. Only common-place surroundings—the trim terraces standing in the distance, the groups of well-dressed children and their nurses—all commonplace enough, and the two young people, Nellie and Lord Seaforth, as commonplace as the rest.

"A pretty girl and a good-looking young man, making love to each other," thought or said the good-natured passers-by; and the ill-natured ones smiled sourly, their day for such pastime being over, or ended in disappointment, or perhaps not come.

A pretty girl in a white dress, and a black cape, and with a fair, sweet, winning face. So fair that Lord Seaforth standing there, looking at her lilies and roses, was moved to a depth of deeper feeling than had ever before passed through his early-worn heart.

"You are very lovely, Nellie," he said, "very lovely and lovable." And he held both her hands tightly in his.

"If you love me really, I care for nothing

more," answered Nellie, in her sweet, modest way. "Why should we think of being married yet? I do not care how long I wait—for years and years."

"Years, my dear child! Where shall I be in years? No, Nellie, we must be married now, or we shall have to part."

"We cannot part," said the girl, speaking very earnestly, and turning pale.

"No, we cannot part," repeated Lord Seaforth. "Now listen to me, my darling. What I propose is—well, I think it would be best to be married in Scotland, and we could live there on the quiet till things blow over a bit. Don't speak for a minute, Nellie. It isn't from any pride or any folly of that kind I wish to keep things quiet. It is simply that if some troublesome acquaintance of mine knew I had married a penniless lassie, they would be down upon me at once, and I would have to bolt —to become, in fact, a ruined, disgraced man— a bankrupt, or worse. If the little woman loves me as she says she does, would she like to bring all this about my ears?"

"Oh, Murray!" And Nellie's eyes filled with tears.

"Don't!" said Lord Seaforth. "Don't look at me like that, child. Perhaps it would be the best thing for you, Nellie, to say good-bye to me, if you can?"

"But I can't—how could I?" answered Nellie, the tears now rolling down the smooth, pink cheeks.

"I am a selfish brute, I daresay," said Seaforth. "All men are selfish, you know, Nell. I ought, of course, to say 'Good-bye, sweetheart,' go and be happy with someone else—some happy dog with more pence than debts. Shouldn't I now, instead of saying— well, all the romantic things I have been saying—eh, Nellie?" And Lord Seaforth laughed.

"I don't think you have been saying anything very romantic," retorted Nellie, rather indignantly, now drying her tears.

"Haven't I? Well, don't look angry. I meant it at least. Nellie, all my life I have had no romance till I met you. That's truth at least—if I'm selfish it's because I love you well."

What did the girl answer? A loving, innocent girl, who knew very little or nothing of

the world? Margaret, with her proprieties, and
her art studies, and—recently—her warm affection for Vyner, had left Nellie very much to
herself. This true and tender heart, therefore,
naturally endowed the man she loved with
every perfection. Seaforth was not only good-
looking in Nellie's eyes, but noble, high-minded,
and true. The wiser Margaret could see errors
even where she loved. But Nellie saw none,
and there was no one to point them out to her
over-partial eyes.

Still, " for father's sake," she would give no
positive answer to her lover's proposal. But
she did not refuse it. How could she—"I who
love him so dearly "—she thought, glancing at
the good-looking face, which somehow looked
more sad than cynical there beneath the trees
on the summer day with sweet Nellie Blythe.

CHAPTER XIV.

MARGARET'S DECISION.

ANOTHER day passed, and still Vyner did not call on his betrothed Margaret. His betrothed Margaret, after mentally deciding that it was quite time that he should do so, wrote him a note, in her clear, firm handwriting, to remind him of his duty, "as I feel a little anxious, dear Walter, that things should be settled now."

Vyner read these words, and then went and stood, pale and deeply moved, before the picture of his Eve. He truly loved Nora Trelawn! It was no brief fancy—not one of those light attractions which come and go, leaving no mark on many a human heart. No; he loved her— dearly loved her—but his honour bound him in galling chains to Margaret, and he felt only that Margaret could set him free.

He had made up his mind to tell Margaret

the story of his early love. Even this had cost
a hard struggle in his heart. A man knows well
enough when a woman loves him, and Vyner
knew that the usually placid, composed Margaret
loved him well. He had been her only lover,
for one thing; for another, Margaret was proud
of his position as an artist; and last, not least,
his handsome face had won her heart.

But Margaret did not worship Vyner with
unreasoning worship. She knew his faults;
speculating in her calm, self-confident way how
it would be best to cure them; feeling quite
sure she would cure them, and that the day
would come when Vyner would be everything
that she wished him to be.

Vyner, of course, did not know all the good
that was in store for him. He only knew that
Margaret Blythe was a handsome young woman
to whom he was engaged, but whose nature was
not akin to his own. But in spite of this want
of kinship, the idea of giving her pain was very
bitter to him. Besides, she might mistake his
motive. Nora's great wealth and her great
poverty made the position doubly trying. Still,
for Nora's sake—yes, for Nora's sake—the man
whispered to his heart, trying to take courage,

as his trembling hand rung that night at the house-door of his betrothed Margaret.

Margaret received him very affectionately. Vyner looked pale, almost grim. He had been hardening his heart as he came along the streets to undergo a scene. He felt that he was going to say a most galling thing to a woman who was a good woman, and worthy of better treatment from his hands. When Margaret kissed his cold cheek, he felt like Judas. When she put her little caressing hand in his, and sat down by his side, he felt he was acting like a scoundrel.

How to begin such a story! Easy is it to say I will do this or that—I will tell this painful truth or the other—but it is not easy to commence words that we know will inflict a stab. Vyner sat silent, pale, biting his lips, trying in vain to speak the words he wanted to say. Margaret herelf at last approached the subject of their marriage with smiling confidence.

"Well, Walter dear," she said, "have you settled anything yet? I have felt a little anxious to know, naturally, during the last two days."

Then Vyner rose from his seat, so visibly agitated that Margaret could not help noticing it.

"Is there anything the matter?" she asked, rather nervously.

"I have something to tell you," answered Vyner, not looking at her—"something that I think it is right you should know, Margaret; mind, I don't wish to influence you—I leave it in your hands—still I will tell you—"

"Is there any reason I should know?" said Margaret, her usually calm voice not a little disturbed. "If—if it is anything that happened, Walter, before I knew you, I would rather not hear it, if it is anything painful."

"It is painful—most painful—it happened before I knew you," said Vyner, forcing himself to speak the unpalatable words. "It happened years ago, Margaret—six years ago—when I was a younger man—"

"I do not wish to hear it," again interrupted Margaret, and her face flushed, for she mistook Vyner's words.

"I would not have told you," continued Vyner, still with averted eyes, "if the happiness of another person was not concerned. For myself—for the sake of my own feelings—I would not have told you. But, Margaret, six years ago I—I cared very deeply for a young girl I then wished to make my wife."

"Walter, what motive can you have for saying this to me?" said Margaret, with some sharpness of tone. "You are bound to me now. Why bring up this old story?"

"Still it is right you should know. Well, six years ago, then, Nora Sudely, now Mrs. Trelawn, was very dear to me—"

"She is very rich, is she not?" said Margaret, yet more coldly, as Vyner paused.

"Yes, she is very rich," said Vyner, and his pale face flushed for a moment, "but her riches or her poverty have nothing to do with it. She was not rich six years ago, when I met her as a young girl at Warbrooke. I was a poor man, then, too, Margaret," and Vyner tried to smile, "and in no position to marry—but I cared for Nora, and I believe my regard was returned, and after she went to live with her aunt, Lady Stainbrooke, I sought her out for the purpose of asking her to wait for me. But her aunt, Lady Stainbrooke—a wicked, worldly, lying Anglo-Indian—invented a vile story to part us. She told Nora I was about to be married to another girl, and Nora believed her and married Mr. Trelawn."

"He left her a great fortune, did he not, quite lately?" said Margaret, whose voice had now grown calm, but a little hard.

"Yes, I believe so—but you will do me the justice, I suppose, to believe that I am not thinking of her money?"

"Yes, Walter, I quite do you that justice. I think it honourable also of you to tell me all this—though I do not quite see your motive for doing so. I honour and respect you too much for a moment to believe that you would think of forsaking the girl to whom you are engaged—to whom you are so soon to be married – for the sake of a rich widow, though you may have had an early liking for this Mrs. Trelawn. Even—if my feelings were nothing—" and again Margaret slid her hand into Vyner's cold, quivering one.

"Then—you wish our engagement to continue?" he asked, in a strange, forced voice.

"Walter! how can you ask such a thing?" answered Margaret, and she hid her face upon his breast.

The manliness, perhaps the tenderness, of his heart made him only feel pity for Margaret at this moment. What right had he, indeed, to feel anything else? Believing Nora was lost to him for ever, he had asked Margaret to be his wife. Because Mr. Trelawn had happened to die, had he any right to play fast and loose with Margaret's affection? He knew that he had none, and he admitted this to himself while Margaret's head lay pillowed on his breast.

Then he moved slightly, and Margaret lifted her head.

"I thought," she said, "instead of telling me this—this painful story—that to-night, Walter, you would have fixed something definite about the time of our marriage. It is so wearing to a girl—and—"

"Settle it when you like," said Vyner, the grim, cold look once more returning to his face; and Margaret smiled, and still held his hand.

"Shall I?" she said. "Very well, Walter; then we must think of a house, you know?"

. . . .

When Vyner returned to his rooms that night, he sat down and wrote a few words to

Nora Trelawn. Nora down at Roseland, living among her flowers, had grown during the last two days to hate their brightness. The mocking sun fell on the river, the mocking sun fell on the roses, but there was no light in Nora's heart—only silent, desolate suspense—sometimes despair.

No letter from Vyner! So three days passed, and she could bear it no longer. Then she proposed to her uncle, Sir Thomas, to return to town; and that ancient warrior—heartily sick of the place, too, by this time—eagerly acceded to her wishes.

"By Jove! the old woman was right, after all," he said. "One would get moss-grown living in a place like this too long!"

So Nora and Sir Thomas returned together to Nora's house at South Kensington. Here they found Lady Stainbrooke, who had been entertaining her friends, courting her neighbour, Lady Seaforth, and altogether enjoying herself.

She received Nora exactly as if no little unpleasantness had ever occurred between them. She had, indeed, taken herself to task for getting out of temper with "the foolish child," as she called Nora, at Roseland.

"So," thought the worldly-wise old woman,
"our handsome painter has got into some
trouble, I suppose, during the five years of
Nora's married life, and he has been forced to
tell her this, and I was called a wicked, lying
old woman in consequence."

Here Lady Stainbrooke chuckled to herself, for,
as we have seen, she had got over her little temper.

"A good thing," she thought, "a very good
thing. Absurd, with Nora's fortune, to think
of marrying a painter."

But to her ladyship's surprise and discomfort
Nora did not seem to have got over her little
temper. She spoke, indeed, so coldly to her
aunt, that Lady Stainbrooke thought that her
dignity required her to remove, for the present
at least, from Nora's house.

Nora made no objection to this plan when
her aunt—at first—rather faintly-hinted her
intention.

Then her ladyship got a little warm again.

"I do not know what has happened to you,
Nora!" she said. "If you have quarrelled
with Mr. Vyner, I certainly have had nothing
to do with your quarrel—yet you treat me
with rudeness—absolute rudeness."

"I have not quarrelled with Mr. Vyner," answered Nora, her pale face flushing as she spoke. "I never quarrelled with him, aunt— as you well know."

"Then why, my dear child, do you make yourself unpleasant to me?"

Nora made no answer. She was not going to bandy any further words with Lady Stainbrooke; but she did not ask her to stay any longer under her roof. Lady Stainbrooke accordingly removed herself to Buckstone for a time, and took her rheumatic General with her.

"Never again," she screamed in her General's ear, as they drove from Nora's house, "shall I endeavour to do any good to anyone! Look how Nora has treated me! I who *made* her —absolutely *made* her—to be insulted for the sake of a painter!"

"You shouldn't have interfered, madam," answered the General. "Men do not care to be interfered with; I don't."

Lady Stainbrooke shrugged her shoulders with an expressive shrug, and then relapsed into silence, brooding as she proceeded on her journey on the general ingratitude of the human race, and the particular ingratitude of Nora Trelawn.

Nora Trelawn felt more low-spirited and miserable than ever after her aunt and uncle had left her. Vyner's letter had followed her to Roseland on the very day of her return to town, and thus was delayed another day before it reached her.

Her neighbour, Lady Seaforth, called upon her, and the clever woman of the world instantly perceived that something unusual was oppressing Nora. These days of suspense had made her look years older than she had done before she went to Roseland.

At last, when four days had elapsed since her painful interview with Vyner, the letter that he had written on his return home, after he had told Margaret Blythe the story of his old love, was placed in Nora's hands.

Ah, poor Nora! Only a few cold, sad words:—

I have seen M. B., and told her how it was with us long ago, but she does not wish to break off her engagement, and I cannot. Nora, what more can I write? I would like to see you, but what could I say? I should never have gone near you. Will you forgive me for having done so, and may God bless and keep you always, and in this to me most bitter hour. W. D. V.

Nora read the painter's miserable words, and then, literally and truly in the emphatic language of old, she "turned her face to the wall." What had she to live for now, she thought, when all the love and light of her life had suddenly passed away into utter darkness?

CHAPTER XV.

MARGARET BLYTHE having obtained Vyner's consent to settle the time of their marriage when she liked, at once began to make energetic preparations for that event.

She had only very little money for her purpose, and to add a trifle more she pinched the already meagrely-provided household almost to starvation.

Nellie naturally noticed this, but she said nothing. Hatton, however, considered it her duty to give her mistress a hint.

" I'm getting that thin, miss," said this oblique-eyed handmaiden, putting her hand as usual on her hip, "that you can count each rib, like a 'maciated greyhound."

" I am sorry you are getting thin, Hatton,"

replied Margaret ; " perhaps if you took oatmeal porridge you might improve."

" Don't think it would 'gree with me, miss," said Hatton, " but perhaps a little more meat would."

But Margaret turned a deaf ear to Hatton's " hint." There were certain dresses that she must have, she decided, before her marriage, and to get these the most rigid household economy was required. But Margaret was careful and clever, and as she cut and contrived her wedding garments she scarcely noticed how pale and stern her promised bridegroom looked, or how the blooming colour had waned on the cheeks of her fair young sister.

Full of herself and her own prospects, Margaret Blythe worked cheerfully on, but at the same time she did not forget the scheme that she had proposed to her father about his future and Nellie's.

She, of course, had to ask Vyner's consent for the Major to live with them—in case of Nellie's marriage—before she could propose to make any formal arrangement on the subject. Any woman with keener susceptibilities would have noticed the half start and the frown with which Vyner received her request. But if Margaret observed these signs of emotion she never guessed their real cause.

"Walter, I have a great favour to ask you. If Nellie marries, may my dear father share our home?" said Margaret.

Then Vyner started and frowned, for the words "our home" grated harshly on his ears.

"I know many men would object to such an arrangement," continued Margaret; "but I know also, Walter dear, that you are different to most men, and that you will respect my motive for this request. You see, Nellie is almost a child, and if she marries young Mr. Saunders, she naturally will live with the old lady who is so devoted to her son, and thus my father would be left entirely alone."

Vyner now forced himself to smile.

"But is Nellie going to marry young Mr. Saunders?" he asked.

"I hope so; nay, I am almost sure that she will. So if my mind were at rest about my father—"

"My dear Margaret, I do not wish to hurry you to leave him."

Margaret's face flushed.

"Walter, do not trifle," she said. "My father is very dear to me—most dear—dearer on account of his sad affliction; but there is some one who is twenty times dearer—some one that I cannot part with now." And Margaret put her hand softly and tenderly into her betrothed's, and looked at him with the love she truly felt, shining in her eyes.

During the last few days Vyner had been trying to school himself to play the part which he too plainly saw that fate—and his own folly—had allotted to him. He was going to marry Margaret Blythe, he told himself; but though he knew this, he hated to be reminded of the fact.

Thus the words " our home " had grated on his ears. And yet he felt at this moment—with her hand in his—how unjust he was to Margaret. He was not a man who perhaps would have cared to have his father-in-law to live with him under the ordinary conditions of married life. But the fact that he did not love his future wife only made him more gentle and complacent to her wishes.

"If Nellie marries, and you wish your father to live with us," he said, after a few moments' consideration, " of course, my dear Margaret, I shall make no objections—I shall be glad for him to be with you."

Then Margaret expressed her gratitude in many tender words.

"It is like you to say so," she said. "You are always noble, always considerate, my dear, dear Walter, and I am the happiest woman in the world."

Margaret was really happy. If an uneasy feeling crept over her sometimes when she remembered Walter Vyner's confession about Nora Trelawn, she soon threw it off.

"He loves me now," she told herself, "and I know that I can keep his love. All men have had some early fancy or other, but they have but one love, and I am Walter's love— and I will prove worthy of his love—I hope I am worthy of it!"

Poor Margaret! Wrapped in her intense self-appreciation, she never saw Walter's wearied looks, or heard his impatient sighs. Trying to do right, when to do wrong was his heart's desire, Walter Vyner walked on the narrow way with laggard footsteps, looking often lingeringly and sadly back at the broad and pleasant road he had left behind.

But he never sought Nora. No answer had come to his few sad words of almost last farewell, as they both—Nora and Vyner—felt them to be. Nora understood and respected Vyner's motives even amid her own bitter grief. And for a time that grief seemed utterly to crush her life. She fell ill, and Lady Stainbrooke at Buckstone—who was not without her paid informants in Nora's household—heard of her illness, and resolved forthwith to bury her wrongs in the past, and again hasten to her rich niece's side.

In the meanwhile Margaret Blythe was going on industriously with her pinching and stitching. She told her father how pleased Vyner was that he should share " our future home." And then she enlarged to the Major on the great benefits that would accrue to them all if Nellie would make up her mind about " young Mr. Saunders's proposal."

This was Margaret's way. Nellie had, she knew, made up her mind about " young Mr. Saunders's proposal," but as she had not made it up the way that Margaret wished, Margaret quietly ignored Nellie's decision. And she persuaded her father—gradually—to see it in her own light. James Saunders was rich and good-natured, and the Major was poor, blind, delicate, and old.

"I may die any day," he sighed, "and where would my darling be then? I cannot expect Vyner to look after her as well. You are quite right, Margaret, she would be better married."

"I will speak to her, dear father," said Margaret. "I will tell her how happy it will make us all to see her happy. We can all live near each other, and Nellie will, I am sure, come to see you every day. Yes, we must try to settle it."

So Margaret tried to settle it. She began very seriously—

"Nellie, dear," she said, "I want to say a few words to you—very serious words."

Nellie's face flushed, and she looked quickly up.

"Walter and I," continued Margaret, "are getting tired of waiting; and Walter, in the most generous manner, has proposed that our dear father should share our future home. You see, Nellie dear, we are poor, very poor, and this will place my father in an independent and easy position for the rest of his life; and I am sure I need not tell you that I will study his comfort in every way."

Nellie made no answer to this, but her face flushed to a yet deeper bloom.

"He shall be my first consideration, after dear Walter," proceeded Margaret. "So, Nellie dear, only your future makes me anxious now. Of course I cannot ask Walter for my sister to live with me as well as my father. Generous and kind as Walter is, that would be expecting too much, especially when he knows, dear, how excellent an offer of marriage is only waiting for your acceptance."

"You mean James Saunders, I suppose?" said Nellie, with a certain harshness in her voice which was very seldom heard there.

"Yes. His mother was telling me only yesterday that he is quite devoted to you, Nellie, and sometimes gets quite low about you. It is very flattering for so rich a young man, and one so much run after also, to be so devoted, isn't it? You are a fortunate girl, Miss Nellie, I can tell you. But jesting apart, dear, I am so anxious this should be settled, and then there would be nothing to interfere with Walter's happiness and mine."

"Then am I to understand, Margaret, that my father wishes to give up his house—wishes to live with you—and that I only am in the way?" asked Nellie, with quick emotion.

"Dear Nellie, do not put it in that stupid way. I have never told you—what good was it to tell you, and worry a young girl?—all the struggles I have had to keep things straight in the house; and now, when my earnings will be gone, I am sure it would be impossible for you and dear father to get along. Everything costs so much now-a-days, and servants eat so much, and are so extravagant—look at Hatton—that unless one has a good income it is impossible to keep things square. No, Nellie, you must not be selfish. Father does not like to say much to you because he is afraid of hurting your feelings, but he fully agrees with me. And just think how comfortable he will be with no coals to buy, or butchers' bills to pay— nothing in fact to vex or trouble him. And you will live near us too, dear, in the Saunders's nice house, and you can bring dear father luxuries—I am sure you will like that, Nellie—"

But Nellie had turned away her head. Then,

to her sister's dismay, a sharp sob sounded in the room.

"You need not make any further arrangements about me, Margaret," said Nellie, with much indignation in her tone and manner. "If father is tired of keeping me I shall not trouble him long; but don't, please, deceive poor James Saunders any more. That at least isn't fair. I am not going to marry him, and you have no right to lead him to suppose that I am. You have made all arrangements, it seems, without consulting me—and, and—so I need not have worried myself so much." And sobbing bitterly, Nellie hastily quitted the room.

Margaret felt exceedingly annoyed—more than annoyed. But still she hoped Nellie would give in. Nellie, on her part, felt angry and bitterly wounded that her father was ready to let her go—ready to give her up to anyone, so that he might live in comfort in Mr. Vyner's house!

Let us follow the weeping, indignant girl to the little bedroom she called her own. See, she hastily unlocks one of the upper drawers in her humble, small, painted chest, and takes out from its resting-place there the cabinet-sized portrait of a good-looking, fair-haired young man. Murray, Viscount Seaforth—smiling as he now very seldom smiled—was portrayed in this coloured specimen of the photographer's art—Murray, Viscount Seaforth, taken five years ago, in his first uniform, when a light and boyish heart beat beneath the braided jacket.

Nellie kissed the smiling face; pressed the smiling face to her heaving, sob-rent bosom.

"Oh! Murray, my love, my love!" she whispered, "I need not have grieved so for father—need not have vexed you. They want me away, and I will go—go with you, my love, my darling—my only one now on all the earth."

Then she sat down, rocking herself to and fro, the smiling, pictured face still lying on her breast. Loving Lord Seaforth even as she did, to leave her home—to leave her father—seemed a terrible step to take so suddenly to this modest, tender girl. But Margaret had wounded her very deeply. Nellie, quick tempered and sensitive, did not pause to consider that her sister was probably exaggerating their father's wishes to suit her own purpose. She only thought they all wished her away. "And I will go—go—"

wept Nellie, kissing again the smiling pictured
face.

Then she read over once more—perhaps for
the twentieth time—the last words that the
original of this smiling pictured face had sent
her—

When are you going to make up your mind, little Nell
(she read in Lord Seaforth's careless handwriting), and take
your worthless—literally, remember—adorer for better and
for worse? A friend of mine has offered to lend me for a
month or so a shooting lodge, or some sort of house at least,
among the wild Western Highlands. Will you come and
kill the red deer in the forests, and the black game, and fish
for salmon in the mountain streams, my Nellie? Ah, child !
—joking apart—let us go away for a while from the weary
life here, and be together by the blue waters of the lochs,
on which the grand, grey hills picture themselves in a fashion
which should make our finest painters tear their best canvas
in despair. There ! is not that a poetical description, my
rosy-cheeked little love? Come then, let us leave duns,
debts, all sorts of bothers behind ; and we can get the fatal
noose tied in Edinbro' fast enough—only you must not tell,
Nellie. You must never, never tell till I give you leave.
Things may turn out better. Some rich old relation may
die, and leave me his happy heir, &c.; but for the present
you *must* promise to keep things quiet. The world—our
little world—must not know. But little Nellie knows what she
really is—what she will always be—to her own SEAFORTH.

How often she had kissed the scrawl at the
end of this letter in which her Murray had

inscribed his name ! That signature when she first saw it had seemed to part them—his different rank stared her in the face, as it were —but now she felt that no rank could part them. Perhaps she only loved the young man more for having held out his lordly hand to clasp one of hers who came of such low degree !

CHAPTER XVI.

THE EMPTY ROOM.

MARGARET having allowed her sister time to "cool down," as she mentally expressed it, went up to the little bed-room where Nellie slept, for the purpose of trying to make peace.

When Margaret entered the room all signs of recent emotion had vanished from Nellie's face. True, Nellie looked paler than usual, perhaps firmer and more resolved, but Margaret did not notice this. She only saw that Nellie had not been crying lately, and she was very glad to see this.

"I came up to see after you, Nellie dear," began Margaret. "I am afraid I vexed you downstairs; but I am sure if you saw it in a right light you would see it was all for your good."

Then Nellie said, rather quickly—

"Please, Margaret, don't say any more about this to-day. I have got a headache. I don't want to talk any more to-day. Is tea ready downstairs yet?"

"I have just made it," answered Margaret. "Come down, dear, and get some; it will do you good." And Nellie having promised to do so, Margaret went away; but before she returned to the front sitting-room where the tea was standing, Margaret had a word to whisper in her father's ear.

"Father," she said, going into the Major's study, and speaking very softly, lest Nellie should overhear on her way downstairs, "I have spoken to Nellie about her marriage, and also about you living with us; so, please, if she says anything to you be careful what you say. It would be such a happy arrangement for us all if she would agree to it, and of course what you say will have great influence upon her."

"But, Margaret," said the Major, "remember I won't have her forced into anything. If the child likes the young man it is different."

"Of course not forced, father dear; but Nellie is only a young girl, easily influenced one way

or the other, and it would be such a good thing
for her to be well married."

"Yes, but still I should not like to urge her."

"But tell her you wish it, father, if she asks
you," said Margaret, earnestly; and the Major
somewhat unwillingly promised to do this.

But Nellie said nothing to her father when
she came downstairs. She was quieter than
she usually was, and she sat reading, or pre-
tending to read, most of the evening, and not
till she was bidding her father good-night,
when the ever-exemplary Margaret was looking
after the house doors, did Nellie show an
unusual emotion.

Then, as she kissed her father, the old man
drew her closer, and kissed again her soft smooth
cheek. As he did this, Nellie gave a little start
and a quiver.

"Father," she said, the next moment, in a
trembling voice, "is it true what Margaret told
me to-day—that—that—you are thinking of
living with Mr. Vyner when he marries
Margaret?"

"Well, Margaret wishes it, my darling,"
answered the Major. "She thinks it would be
best, and she thinks if you marry, my little girl—"

But Margaret's step was now heard in the passage close to the parlour door, and without another word Nellie lifted up her head, and drew back from her father's arms.

" Good-night, father," she said, quietly, and then went away ; and Major Blythe ever afterwards bitterly regretted that he had allowed her to go.

Indeed, the Major determined in his own mind, after she had left him, that he would shortly come to a fuller understanding with his young daughter. But during the following day he had no opportunity of doing this. Nellie was out the greater part of the morning, and Vyner spent the evening with them, and Nellie and the Major were never alone.

But when Nellie parted with him for the night, the Major grew more determined in his purpose to speak to her. Somehow the old man thought that his little girl's arms clung more tenderly than usual round his neck as she gave him her customary kiss.

" And I want you to give me something to-night, father," she said, as if she were trying to speak jestingly.

" Well, what is it, my little lassie ? "

answered the Major, caressingly, holding her hands.

"Just a little bit, a very little bit of your hair," said Nellie. "May I cut it off now, father?"

"What nonsense, Nellie, to worry father to-night!" said Margaret, who was standing near them by the side of Vyner.

"Father won't mind," said Nellie, in her old pretty, wilful way, and she went and got her scissors, and, stooping over her father, cut off a piece of his iron-grey hair.

"Thank you," she said, and she kissed his forehead. "I will always keep it."

"But why do you want it to-night, Nellie?" asked Margaret.

"I want to put it in a locket," answered Nellie. "Thank you again, father."

"Give me another kiss for it then, darling," said the Major, and then Nellie put her arms round her father's neck, and kissed him very tenderly.

"Good-night, my darling—God bless you," whispered the Major, and somehow he fancied that a tear for a moment wet his cheek.

So impressed was he by Nellie's manner, that

no sooner was Vyner gone, than he spoke seriously to Margaret on the subject.

"My dear," he said, addressing his eldest daughter, when they were alone, "I want to speak to you about Nellie. I don't think the child is happy, and I won't have her teazed or worried about this marriage with young Saunders. If she were fond of him, of course, I would be glad to have her well settled; but if she is not, we must keep on this house, and manage without you as best we can. Nellie's happiness is and must be the first consideration, and I have not been satisfied with her manner these two nights."

"She is a little unsettled perhaps," said Margaret, "that is all; and I am sure, dear father, that it is her true happiness that I also am thinking of."

"Well, dear, I will speak to her in the morning," answered the Major, "and be guided by what she says."

And determined to carry out this idea in spite of Margaret, the Major retired to bed.

The night wore on over the heads of the quiet household. Hour after hour went on to join the past. Then the dawn broke, and up betimes rose Margaret, sitting down steadily to two hours' work at her wedding garments before breakfast time. The Major came down late.

"Nearly ten o'clock, father," said Margaret, in mild reproof, "and Nellie not down yet— I have been up since six."

As Nellie did not appear at a quarter-past ten, Margaret went up to seek her. She knocked at her sister's bedroom door, but there was no response, so Margaret walked unbidden into the room.

She started, almost gave a cry, when she got there. The bed had not been slept in, and there was no Nellie to be seen. There was a certain strangeness, too, in the appearance of the room—scraps of paper, pieces of twine, a dozen little things that told some sort of packing had been going on. Then, as Margaret's startled gaze wandered around, her eyes suddenly fell on a letter lying on the toilet table.

To seize this and read the address was the work of a moment. It was directed to Major Blythe, and Margaret at once opened it, and as she read her young sister's words she grew sick and cold with fear. How could she tell her father? she was thinking; how could she break this dreadful news?

For in her letter Nellie bade her father and sister good-bye.

I am going away to-night, dear father (read poor trembling Margaret), but you must not be uneasy about me if you do not hear of me for a long, long time. Where I am going I shall be well cared for; and as you have settled to live with Margaret and Mr. Vyner, I hope that you will not miss me. But I will not forget my dear, dear father; and I hope my dear, dear father will not forget his little Nell. Some day I will come back to you, father; and till that day comes I will often, often think of you. But do not vex yourself about me; I shall, I hope, be well and happy, and I hope that you will keep well and happy also. Give my love to Margaret.

Your loving and affectionate daughter,

NELLIE.

Margaret read and re-read these words, and her usual self-possession seemed entirely to forsake her. Did she blame herself? No; Margaret never blamed herself—it was not in her nature to do so—but she was greatly shocked and overcome.

While she was standing thus, Nellie's farewell letter grasped in her trembling hand, she heard her father's voice calling from below.

"Is anything the matter with little Nell?" called the Major; and, pale and even faint,

Margaret went down to her father, still holding
Nellie's letter in her hand.

"Is the child not well?" asked the Major,
when he heard his daughter's footsteps approaching him.

Then Margaret took her father's hand, and
led him back into the parlour.

"Father," she said in a faltering voice, "do
not be afraid; Nellie has done a very foolish
thing. I cannot imagine how she could do
such a thing, but—but she is not upstairs."

"Not upstairs!" repeated the Major.
"What do you mean, Margaret? Tell me at
once what you mean?"

"She has left a letter," continued Margaret,
with great emotion, "a letter for you, father.
I have opened it; it is a sort of farewell
letter. Nellie is gone somewhere—but, but we
will find her. Father! father!" And Margaret
caught her father by the arm.

For with a terrible cry the blind man lifted
up his hands when he heard the news.

"Gone!" he cried. "Nellie, my darling,
do you say *gone?* Where has she gone? Have
you done this, Margaret?" he added fiercely.
"Answer me—have you done this?"

" Do not be unjust, father," said Margaret, to a certain extent recovering her self-possession. " I, who have done everything for Nellie—I have done nothing, given her nothing but kindness and love. But I will read her letter."

With a moan, Major Blythe tottered to a seat, and then Margaret read aloud poor Nellie's farewell words. As Margaret concluded, the unhappy father utterly broke down.

" My darling, my darling ! " he sobbed. " Oh, Nellie, how could you leave me—blind and helpless. I cannot try to find you, Nellie—"

" Hush, father," said Margaret, " do not give way thus ; you will be ill if you do, and that will only make matters worse. We must try to find Nellie—we must find her—and we must keep all this quiet, if we can. Let us try to think calmly. What can have been Nellie's motive for this rash, misguided step ? "

Again Major Blythe moaned aloud. The bitterness of his blindness seemed terrible to him at this moment.

" What about this talk of her marriage with young Saunders ? " he said. " I noticed she was not herself lately—and she may have thought, poor—tender-hearted child—that we wished her to marry against her will? In her letter she speaks of my living with you and Vyner, does she not? But I won't, Margaret! I will keep on this house if I starve in it. My child shall have a home to come to, at any rate, whenever she returns."

"We will see about all this, father, by-and-by; but don't excite yourself now. You see, Nellie says in her letter she hopes to be well and happy, and that some day she will come back. Can it be? Can she have married anyone unknown to us? But no, no; she knew no one—no, she has probably gone to some educational establishment or other, that she has seen advertised, as a pupil teacher. Yes; this is the most likely thing I can think of."

"She—she knew Lord Seaforth," said Major Blythe, slowly and painfully.

"Lord Seaforth!" echoed Margaret. "It cannot be, father! And yet—yet—when I think of it, she spoke very sharply to me once in his defence, when I so justly blamed him for coming here, and allowing us to believe he was only Captain Seaforth! If I thought this, father—"

" If I thought this," said the Major, rising passionately from the chair, " blind as I am, I'll force him to marry her! I'll go to his mother's house this very day, and learn the truth ! "

" But we have no proof, father. Still, there is just a probability. He came here a great deal, did he not, at one time ? "

" Yes, at the time of Wallace's accident, when you were staying with your friend at Woolwich. She has seen him since, I know. One day, I remember her telling me he had told her he was Lord Seaforth—"

"And you did not tell me this, father? You did not confide in me, though you know how earnestly I have tried to do my duty to you and Nellie."

The Major was silent. He felt that perhaps he deserved this reproof, for there were many things that he and his little Nellie had not told to Margaret.

" Did she say anything more to you ? " continued Margaret. " At least tell me the truth *now*, father — though it may be too late."

" Nothing. I remember being uneasy when I heard this man was Lord Seaforth. But if he has done anything to the child he shall answer to me for it."

"He lives with his mother," said Margaret, "and his mother lives in one of the South Kensington Squares. I know this because Walter has dined there; and if he has induced Nellie to run away with him, he also will have left home. We must go to his mother, father."

"Let us go now; at once, then."

"Stay, let me think—best keep this as quiet as we can, father, for all our sakes—for Nellie's sake, for Walter's sake, for mine. A woman can do a thing more quietly than a man. Let me go alone to Lady Seaforth's; she knows Walter—that alone will be an introduction."

"Well, if you think so. But be quick, Margaret! How can I wait here—wait helpless here—till you return?"

"Dear father, it is only a remote chance I am going on, so you must not expect too much. Still I think we have some just cause of suspicion, at least if Nellie met Lord Seaforth, as you say, unknown to me?"

This parting reproof being administered, Margaret got ready to start for Lady Seaforth's. She did not rush off in hot haste, but prepared deliberately to encounter her ladyship. As she pinned on her hat and arranged her veil, however, the probability of Nellie having run away with Lord Seaforth grew upon her mind. "This would account for Nellie's otherwise unaccountable rejection of James Saunders's excellent proposal,"thought Margaret. "No one in her senses would have refused such an offer without cause, and I believe now this cause has been Lord Seaforth," at last she decided.

Margaret—ever economical—would not drive the whole way to South Kensington, even though her father urged her to do so. She went so far in the train, and then took a cab, and drove to Lady Seaforth's house. To her surprise, when she rung the door-bell and asked if Lady Seaforth were at home, the footman admitted her at once with a jaunty air and a smile.

"Oh, y're the young lady from—" (and Margaret could not catch the name), said the man. "Come in, and I'll ring for Thompson, the maid, and she'll take you up to my lady."

Margaret immediately saw there was some mistake; but after a moment's consideration, as she stood there in the hall, she determined to take advantage of it. She *must* see Lady

Seaforth, she told herself; and as Lady Seaforth
was evidently expecting some lady, the easiest
way to procure an interview was to pretend
not to notice the footman's error.

In a minute or two Thompson, the maid,
appeared.

"You can come up with me," she said,
addressing Margaret. "I hope you have been
able to match it?"

Then Margaret's face flushed red beneath her
veil, and her very ears began to tingle. She
had been mistaken for some shop girl, some
milliner's girl, she thought angrily, and she
opened her lips to tell the maid her true
position. But Thompson never looked round.
She walked very fast, and Margaret walked
after her, angry and indignant, until they came
to a room door, which the maid pushed open.

"Go in there," she said, "my lady will speak
to you in a moment or two."

How degrading, how annoying, thought
Margaret, who had always prided herself on
looking perfectly lady-like! But though greatly
annoyed, her common-sense told her that the
best thing to do now was to see Lady Seaforth.
So drawing herself up, and trying to look as

dignified as she could, Margaret stood for the
next quarter of an hour. Then she heard two
people outside the door talking in reference to
herself.

"You have not seen it, then?" some one was
saying. "The woman who brought it is here,
isn't she? It must match, Thompson, or it
will spoil the whole effect." And a moment
later the door opened, and a haughty-looking,
fair-haired woman entered.

Margaret did not know Lady Seaforth by
sight, yet she felt sure that this was Lady
Seaforth. The small high features and the
blue eyes reminded her of features and eyes
she had seen before. Lady Seaforth bore a
certain likeness to her son, yet the expression
of their faces was so totally different that it
marred the effect of the features. The haughty,
prominent blue eyes of the mother scarcely
glanced at Margaret as she entered the room.
Margaret bowed, and Lady Seaforth made a
hardly perceptible movement of her head.

"You have brought the lace?" she said. "I
hope it is the exact pattern—nothing else will
do."

"There is some mistake," said Margaret,

trying not to seem nervous. " If you are
Lady Seaforth, I wish to see you. But I have
brought no lace—I have come on a very
different errand."

Then the large, haughty, prominent blue
eyes did look at Margaret.

" I am Lady Seaforth," said her ladyship ;
" but if you have not brought the lace from
Marshall and Snelgrove's, why are you here ?"

" I—I wish to speak to you," answered
Margaret, " and your servants mistook me for
some other person. I—I must speak to you,
Lady Seaforth."

" What can you possibly have to say to me ?"

" It is on a most painful subject," faltered
Margaret, her boasted self-possession all vanish-
ing away before the cold, haughty stare that
the blue eyes had now fixed on her. " I wish
to speak to you—about your son."

" My son ?" repeated Lady Seaforth, in the
coldest accents. " I decline to speak to you
on such a subject. I request that you will
leave the room."

" No ; I must speak to you ! You mistake
me entirely, Lady Seaforth," said Margaret,
eagerly. " I am not a shop girl ; I have brought

no lace ; I am a young lady by birth, and I want to speak to you about my sister."

"I decline, I repeat, to hold any conversation with you," said Lady Seaforth, and she turned to leave the room; but Margaret sprang forward, and stood before her.

"Do not go away, Lady Seaforth," she said, "for a moment or two—not till you have heard what I have got to say, if you would save great scandal and exposure. I am the daughter— one of the daughters—of Major Blythe; and your son, Lord Seaforth, used to visit at our house. I have a young sister—Nellie—Lady Seaforth, do listen to me—Nellie has disappeared from her home—"

"What have I to do with such a story?" interrupted Lady Seaforth.

"Your son knew Nellie—used to meet Nellie," faltered Margaret, "and I want to know—is he at home?"

"Lord Seaforth? Certainly he is at home. What do you mean by such a question?"

"Lady Seaforth," said Margaret, galled to the quick by Lady Seaforth's contemptuous manner, "I think I have some right to ask it. Lord Seaforth came to our house first under a

false name. He called himself Captain Seaforth ;
and as my father is an officer and a gentleman
that was scarcely a right thing to do, was it ?"

"If your father is a gentleman, he should not
have permitted such a thing to happen. But I
have nothing to do with such a question.
Once more I ask you to leave the house."

"You treat me very rudely," said Margaret,
her eyes filling with indignant tears, "yet—yet
I am engaged to a gentleman you ask to dine
here—to Mr. Vyner, the painter."

"I know Mr. Vyner merely as a man of
ability, as a painter—I know nothing of his
belongings," answered Lady Seaforth, with
unchanged coldness.

"He has no reason to be ashamed of his
belongings," retorted Margaret, very angrily.
"But all I can say is, if your son has induced
my sister—"

Upon this Lady Seaforth rang the bell very
loudly, and in a minute later the door opened,
and her maid Thompson looked in.

"Show this person out at once," said Lady
Seaforth ; and what could Margaret do but go ?

Wounded and indignant, scarcely able to
restrain her tears, she followed the maid down-

stairs. The hall door was open, and a charger
with military accoutrements, and held by a
groom, was pawing the ground impatiently
before the door. As Margaret went out of the
vestibule she saw why the horse was waiting.

Leaning against a carriage which was standing before the door of the next house was a tall,
slender figure in an officer's undress uniform.
In a moment Margaret recognised him—the
delicate profile, the light hair—it was Lord
Seaforth ; and Margaret started and half-
stopped.

Should she speak to him ? she was thinking.
But even as the thought passed through her
mind his light laugh fell on her ears. Then
she looked at the lady in the carriage to whom
he was talking.

She saw a pale woman with dark, sad eyes,
dressed in black. Where had she seen that
face ? She had seen it somewhere, Margaret
knew, but at the moment could not recall
where. But she felt that it was impossible
to address Lord Seaforth while he was talking
to this lady. So she was forced to pass on,
having gained the knowledge, however, to take
to comfort her father, that Lord Seaforth had

certainly not run away with Nellie, as he was still living in his mother's house.

As Margaret went home she remembered where she had seen the lady's face. It was in Vyner's studio—the face of the picture called " *His Eve.*"

CHAPTER XVII.

CHOOSING A HOUSE.

PACING to and fro in the little parlour, racked with the cruelest anxiety, Major Blythe had spent the time which had been passed in so humiliating a manner by Margaret.

Then, when he heard his daughter's returning footsteps, he groped his way eagerly into the passage.

"Well," he asked breathlessly, as he met Margaret; but for a moment Margaret was so worried and annoyed that she made no reply.

"Have you heard anything?" asked the trembling old man, and Margaret looked up at her father's sharpened face, and answered quickly—

"She has not run away with Lord Seaforth, father—I saw him in his uniform at his mother's door."

"And did you see Lady Seaforth? Did you ask her anything?"

"I saw her for a few minutes," said Margaret, ashamed to confess her bitter humiliation, "and she told me her son was at home—that is all. I said as little as possible, for all our sakes. I repeat, this is best kept as quiet as we can."

"But am I to sit down and lose my child without making an effort to find her?" asked Major Blythe, indignantly. "I won't do it, Margaret! Nellie must be somewhere, and I shall at once apply to the police."

"Then everyone will know."

"What is everyone to me in comparison to Nellie? I must find her; I will find her; so you need not attempt to prevent me doing so."

Upon this Margaret burst into tears. Never had she felt so cruelly injured. All her life at home she had been looked up to and respected, and her will had been almost absolute law. She had thought herself the incarnation of all womanly virtues, and the Major and her sister had never attempted to differ openly from the opinion she held of herself. And to be insulted thus! First to feel powerless, to be tamed, held in awe, as it

were, by Lady Seaforth's cold blue eyes, and
then to be told by her father that she need not
attempt to prevent him trying to find Nellie!

"I have not deserved this," wept Margaret;
and her father was obliged to beg her pardon,
and to praise her and propitiate her, before
Margaret would attempt to be comforted.

She felt really very unhappy, for she was so
afraid of the effect that the news of Nellie's
flight might have on Vyner. She never
understood Vyner. The effect of the news of
Nellie's flight was exactly contrary to what she
feared. The painter, large and generous,
whatever his faults might be, drew naturally
nearer to the weeping woman in her hour of
trouble.

He was touched, he was sorry, he kissed
Margaret's tear-stained cheeks, as he had never
kissed them in their usual smooth and admir-
able condition.

"Poor little Nell! Poor foolish child!" he
said. He did not reproach Margaret with her
abortive scheme to marry little Nell to young
Saunders, though he was pretty well satisfied
in his own mind that this was really the cause
of the poor girl's flight. He said only kind

words to Margaret, and Margaret—still not understanding him—began to smile again, satisfied that Vyner loved her too much, appreciated her many virtues too highly, to permit any family disgrace to come between them.

Sad, is it not, to live with those, to be tied to those, to whom, indeed, we have no tie? Between Margaret and Vyner there was a great gulf; but Margaret's understanding was not large enough to perceive this. She thought Vyner had peculiar ideas sometimes, a man of vagrant moods, perhaps, like most artists; but she did not see—could not understand, in fact —the great difference between them.

Had Margaret told Vyner—she carefully did not—how Lady Seaforth had spoken of him, he would but have laughed. He knew why her ladyship had asked him to dinner, and how she regarded him. He knew also how he regarded her, though she might think herself a great lady; but to be great in Vyner's eyes needed something better than a name, however high sounding, that would be writ only on a crumbling tombstone.

So Margaret dried her tears, and Vyner did

what he could to comfort her, and also to
comfort the old man in his sore distress. But
the father's grief was very different to Margaret's.
Margaret had her lover, her approaching marriage, to think of, but Major Blythe had nothing
now to lighten his long dark hours. He had
been cheerful and content enough—as most
blind people are—before Nellie disappeared,
but it was very pitiful now to see his restless
sorrow.

Four days passed on, and nothing was heard
of Nellie. Vyner applied to the police, and
inquiries were made, and the neighbours heard,
and there was a talk and a scandal, but nothing
was discovered. Nellie had vanished, gone out
in the night somewhere, taking very little with
her, leaving—she little guessed—how miserable
and anxious a heart behind!

The manner of her flight from the house was
very easily explained. Margaret always locked
the doors herself, and took the small basket
containing the keys with her into her own
room. The front house door-key was found in
the lock the morning Nellie's disappearance was
discovered. Thus Nellie must have entered
her sister's room when Margaret was asleep,

and taken the key from the basket, and opened
the door. Margaret declared this to be impossible, she slept so lightly, &c. ; but the fact
remained the same, and there could indeed be
no reasonable doubt about the matter.

No one appeared to have seen Nellie leave
her father's house, and not a human soul came
forward to give any account of her. Vyner
saw Lord Seaforth a few days afterwards in the
park, and the young lord smiled and nodded to
the painter. It seemed impossible, therefore,
to the Blythes, any further to attempt to trace
Nellie's flight as being in any way connected
with Lord Seaforth. Nellie had never spoken
of him as her lover ; had never told how often
she had met him; and gradually the idea faded
out of Margaret's mind. Margaret finally
believed that Nellie, for some strange fancy or
other, had gone out as a pupil teacher, or
perhaps to other employment, and she was for
ever telling her father that she was sure Nellie
would soon tire, and then she would return to
her home.

But the summer faded into the autumn, and
still nothing was heard of Nellie. Then Margaret began to speak again to Vyner of their

marriage. During all the time of their grief
and anxiety, she had gone on with her stitching
and pinching. It occupied her mind, she told
poor weeping, sympathising Mrs. Saunders,
who was grieving sorely for her James's disappointment. Mrs. Saunders took a worse
view of the case than Margaret. She believed
"the sweet, pretty young creature" had come
to an untimely end. She had gone mad,
perhaps, she thought, and had wandered out,
and might now be lying amid the chill slime
in the river's bed.

"And with such chances, too, as she had,"
sighed Mrs. Saunders, thinking of her beloved
son. "My James was that fond of her, he
would have married her to-morrow! Ay, we
never can tell. The best and the best loved
are took first, Miss Margaret. This world's a
queer jumble, but perhaps in the next, things
will be put straight a bit."

Poor little Puck (James Saunders) was really
terribly "cut," as he expressed it, about
Nellie's disappearance. The brandy and soda
that he had swallowed to console himself was
something terrible, and his eyes were con-
tinually blood-shot, perhaps with tears. He

inclined to his mother's gloomy views about
Nellie.

"No girl in her senses would have done
it!" he was wont to say. "I would have married her. Can a fellow do more? Would a
girl in her right mind have run away when she
had such a chance? No; the poor darling must
suddenly have become insane, and perhaps
fancied all sorts of things—perhaps that I
wasn't going to behave well to her—there is
no saying when the brain is upset what people
will think. Mother, can it be in the family,
do you think? The Major's blind—that's
queerish; there's some connection, isn't there,
between the eyes and the brain?"

"Don't know, my darling," answered the
meek, fond mother. "If your dear father had
been alive he would have told us; but I never
went much into the sciences."

"Nor I," truthfully affirmed James; and so
in this simple fashion they talked of poor
Nellie, it being more consoling to James's
feelings to believe her dead or insane, than the
idea that she had run away when she had a
chance of marrying him.

But all this time, though there was no trace

or sign of Nellie, Margaret steadily went on making her marriage garments. In spite of her father's grief and anxiety she did this; in spite indeed of her own anxiety. But when she spoke to her father on the subject, to her pain and annoyance she found the old man held to his first determination, made after Nellie's flight, and would not now hear of living with herself and Vyner.

"No, the child shall have a home to come to, however poor it may be," he said. "Don't attempt to persuade me, Margaret. As long as I'm alive, I'll keep the house waiting for Nellie."

"But, father dear, just think, how can you manage?" said the careful daughter. "You could not afford to pay a regular housekeeper, and they are so dreadfully extravagant, even if you could—it will be impossible for you to manage."

"I'll keep a home for Nellie," persisted Major Blythe; and when Margaret, having used all the arguments in her power without avail, asked Vyner to try to persuade him, Vyner told her that he thought the Major was right.

"How do we know where she is, Margaret?" he said. "Perhaps nearer than we think; and if she knew—if she heard that her father was alone, she might come to him. I think you are wrong to try to persuade your father against his will. If you do not like to leave him, we can wait?"

But Margaret would not hear of this.

"No," she said, "no, Walter! I am weary of waiting—surely it is time we took a house? You do not hesitate, do you, Walter, on account of this sad affair about poor Nellie?"

"You know I do not," answered the painter, sharply and coldly. He was stung that she should suggest such a thing—stung and indignant.

"Then you will look for a house at once, dearest?" softly said Margaret; and Vyner promised, and sick at heart, the next day started on that dreary search.

In all Margaret's confidences to her betrothed —and she was very tender to him—she had never told him that she had, she was convinced, seen the original of the picture that he called *My Eve*, talking in her carriage to Lord Seaforth. But Margaret had, nevertheless,

thought a good deal about this incident. She
had learned that Mrs. Trelawn, Vyner's old
love, the rich widow, lived next door to Lady
Seaforth. The carriage in which she had seen
the lady that Vyner's hand had, she was sure,
portrayed in *My Eve*, was standing before this
very door. Then the lady was dressed in black
—in mourning—and looked years and years
older—so Margaret decided—than the bright,
smiling, dark-eyed woman whom Vyner had
painted. So Margaret concluded that he had
painted this portrait in Mrs. Trelawn's girlhood, when—"he had admired her"—Margaret
mentally called it; but somehow this meeting
with the dark-eyed lady, whose picture was in
Vyner's studio, had a little disturbed Margaret.
So much so that she never mentioned it to
Vyner; so much so that she was more anxious
than ever to marry Vyner. The dark-eyed woman
was only a youthful dream, " and all men have
their follies," she told herself, but still Margaret
was very anxious to have her marriage over,
and to have that youthful dream for ever left
behind.

Therefore she urged him to look for a house;
and Vyner went. To look out for a house is

not a pleasant task. To walk up carpetless
stairs, gaze into empty rooms, examine cloudy
cornices, is not, as a rule, an agreeable office,
even if love be there to warm the heart with
dreams of a sweet future, in the now dull
and dusty space !

But what when love is not there? Our
supposed lover—unhappy Vyner—said not to
himself after tramping up the carpetless stairs,
as he gazed into the dusty rooms, "My
Margaret will make all this bright; my
Margaret will sit there; my Margaret,—"
&c., &c. Why go on with a lover's endless
fancies? They are sweet visions these, fulfilled
or unfulfilled; they make an Eden again on
earth for a brief, brief season. The sunshine
falls on the empty rooms as the fond lover
walks through them. But a London fog seemed
to accompany our poor Vyner. It was a weary,
heavy task, and at last Vyner threw it up.

Every house he thought of, Margaret objected
to in her gentle, determined way. One was
too small, the other too large. One looked
north, and would be too cold; the other south,
and would be too hot.

"May I go, dear Walter, and see what I can

do, since it seems to worry you so?" asked
Margaret; and Vyner was only too glad to
give his consent.

After this, the question of the house, we may
be sure, was very soon settled. Hope and love
accompanied Margaret in her peregrinations,
and she went very briskly about with these
two companions. She settled on a house, and
she took Vyner to see it. He made some faint
objections, but she overruled them.

"I see I shall be henpecked," he said, with
rather a rueful smile, which Margaret answered
by a proud, confident one.

But he knew all the while that he would not
be "henpecked." He gave in to Margaret
because he could not be at the trouble, because
his heart felt too weary to contend with her,
and not because he was afraid of her. He
would never be afraid of her. He knew this,
and he knew also he would never love her.
But he was bound by honour. How often
had he said this to himself, and he said it
again, looking at her in the dusty rooms of
the empty house in which these two proposed
to live!

But they took the house. Then Vyner gave

Margaret a sum of money, and she furnished the house. Furnished the house—let us do her justice—with taste and discretion. Margaret had a sense and appreciation of beauty, and she chose her colours well. Even Vyner admitted this, though his new possessions gave no pleasure to his eyes.

CHAPTER XVIII.

THE OLD ROMANCE.

ALL this while, when Margaret was stitching and furnishing, a cold grey shadow lay over the life of Nora Trelawn.

She had been very ill—a nameless illness. "Want of tone," the doctors said. "Utter folly," thought her aunt, Lady Stainbrooke. But all the same this illness had brought her very low, and her beauty had faded, and her dark eyes were violet-rimmed, heavy, and sad.

She was wounded—bitterly wounded—because Vyner had never sought her since he had told her in his letter that he was bound by honour to fulfil his engagement to Margaret Blythe. Even if he were bound to fulfil his engagement—and Nora admitted that in this he was but right and honourable, though it was breaking *her* heart—but even if he were bound to fulfil his engagement, need he utterly turn away from his old friend? So, woman-like, argued Nora. She would rather have seen him at any cost. Even "heart-wrung tears," shed in his presence, seemed to her to be better than this cold silence and absence. She did not know—how could she?—that more than once Vyner had stood outside, and looked up at the lighted windows of her house with strange tenderness and bitter regret swelling in his heart.

One night from her drawing-room windows —he standing in the street below—he heard the fresh pure voice of a girl singing. This song seemed to smite him as with bodily pain. What! was he forgotten, then—was she having singing and merriment—and he—and he? Then Vyner turned away, and went back to his Margaret. He smiled grimly to himself as he sat by his Margaret's side, knowing that she never noticed his cold abstraction. She was not thinking of him, but of her new dresses, and her new furniture.

"Yet she is not a bad woman," thought Vyner; "only a great thick wall is growing thicker and thicker each day between our hearts."

What was cementing this wall was no doubt
Vyner's love for another woman. Margaret
would have been more pleasing in his sight—
for she was certainly good-looking—if the soft,
dark eyes of another woman had not told him
of the tender, wistful love he was forced to put
away. He was always comparing her mentally
with Nora Trelawn. Margaret's self-assertiveness jarred on him when he remembered Nora's
sweet humility and softness. Nora was very
womanly—full of womanly faults, perhaps ;
but faults are sometimes more pleasing than
virtues, when virtues are too unsparingly
presented to our gaze.

"But Nora has forgotten me," thought Vyner,
bitterly, sitting by Margaret's side. " Well
—it is better so." Yet this idea was not
consoling to him. Margaret's self-assertiveness
jarred upon him more than ever that night.
Hearing of his new furniture, of the colour of
the dado in his drawing-room, was dust and
ashes to his ears. He went home early ; life
was not worth living for, he decided, with its
endless worries, its struggles between duty and
inclination, between right and wrong.

He was weary of it all, in fact—the dark

spirit was upon his soul ; some envious fellow
had said his last picture was bad, and a friend
had whispered the adverse opinion to him.
Everything was going wrong, and so, heart-sick
and sad, Vyner sat by his fire, thinking—
enviously—that unmarried men at least can
have the privilege of being sometimes alone.

He went to his work next day, heavy and
uninterested. Yet he had loved his work, and
still loved it. He would live for it again, he
told himself—thrusting away his weary thoughts
—as he had lived for it in the past years, when
Nora Trelawn was Mr. Trelawn's wife, and he
had no love but one that was dead and buried
to worry him.

And as he painted on he forgot Margaret,
and his new furniture, and his new house. He
went out from his real to an ideal world. He
was standing on the wintry shore, and the
sound of the wild sea was breaking on his ears
as he painted it dashing against the jagged
rocks, and carrying home the dead sailor whose
wife was waiting and watching.

Vyner was a true artist. The passions that
he portrayed passed through his heart. His
sensitive, nervous hand never could, and never

would, he used to say, draw what his brain and soul had seen before he sat down to his canvas. He knew his power, but with the humility which came of true self-knowledge, was ever ready to admit how often he failed, how often his work was wanting in his sight.

But he would live for it, he said again; and so after a hard day's labour he went out to have a turn in the Park, late in the afternoon of the day following the one on which he had sat by his Margaret's side, and thought sadly enough that Nora Trelawn had utterly forgotten him.

The Park was very empty. The season was quite over, and only a few carriages were to be seen. Vyner never looked at the carriages. He went striding on thinking—absolutely of that dark-eyed woman still—when suddenly he looked up, and there, sitting in a passing carriage with a grey-haired, bent man by her side, actually was Nora!

He started, he stopped, and stared at the carriage, but Nora never saw him. But he saw her—saw the sweet face changed and wasted, and the dark eyes violet-rimmed, heavy, and sad. Then he knew he was not forgotten;

grief was on Nora's face and weariness; the weariness that he remembered to have seen there in her wedded days, when he had met her long ago, and told her that Lady Stainbrooke had spoilt their lives.

Was he glad to see the shadow again on Nora's face? Was life as burdensome to him as it had been last night when he turned away from Nora's lighted windows? Strange, the man who loved her so, felt more bright of mood after he had seen that clouded countenance. He was not forgotten. He would go back to his work, and she would be proud of him even if their hands never met again on earth. Yes; he was not forgotten, and the thought was balm and comfort to Vyner's soul.

He knew the old man, too, who sat by her side. That pale, pinched face, carried his memory back to Warbrooke; back to the days when he had wooed Nora in the Warbrooke meadows. It was Mr. Henry Sudely, Nora's father, for Lady Stainbrooke had advised her brother to come and pay his rich daughter a visit, as she " wanted rousing."

Poor Mr. Sudely was not of a very " rousing " nature. Sitting in his rich daughter's carriage,

living in her fine house, the old shadows still
hung over him. He had been "too beaten by
the world," too battered by its rude shocks,
ever to forget them. He had failed ; had to
face angry, insulting creditors ; he had scarcely
known where to turn for daily bread ; he had
struggled and struggled, and then a young
girl's marriage had changed it all.

But the "hard times" had left their mark.
It seemed impossible to Mr. Sudely to be lively
and light-hearted. The storm-worn old ship
might be fresh painted and rigged, but the
leaks were below the paint. Mr. Sudely had
plenty now, but he never could quite forget
the days when the wolf was at the door, and
when shame and dishonour had stalked by his
side.

Thinking of these old days, Vyner went home.
The old romance, the old love, all came freshly
back to him. He turned the face of his pictured
Eve again from the wall, and there before him
was Nora—the Nora he had wooed in the
Warbrooke meadows.

Then he felt a strange longing, a longing
that grew upon him day by day, once more to
see Roseland. He remembered the touch of

the soft hand there holding the flower, and the sweet glad face of Nora standing in the sunlight.

"I am a fool," he told himself, and yet he went to have a last look at the rose garden by the river. He went on a cold dull day, the river dark and rough, and before he reached Nora's house rain began to fall heavily, and the wind swept by with a wintry chill.

He thought of turning back; but no—he would not perhaps have cared to see Roseland again in the glory of the sunshine, as it had been on the day when he had stood with Nora by the garden wall. He would go on, and he went on, and when at length he arrived, he found to his surprise the gate of the avenue standing open. He went through the gate and down into the garden. He did not mean to go near the house, or speak to the servants in charge of it, unless they spoke to him. He meant— "fool that I am," he said again to himself—to lean for a moment or two on the little stone balustrade where he had leaned with Nora; he meant to pluck a rose, perhaps, and then—let us hope—go back with a lighter heart to his work and to his Margaret, and to the life that now so plainly lay mapped before him.

But let us follow him down the wet paths among the faded roses. He looked sadly and grimly at the flowers. Dashed by the wind and rain, out of season, drooping and melancholy, stood the rose trees. Then he looked for the moss-grown wall at the end of the garden. He looked and stood still; a thrill, a sudden bodily pang, darting to his heart.

There—leaning against the very stones where they too had leaned in the sunshine— her head down, the rain beating on her black dress—was Nora Trelawn! Vyner's breath came short for a moment or two, his face flushed; then a sudden glow of love, passion, and regret swept over him, and with quick, uncertain steps he went on.

Nora heard the footsteps behind her, and lifted her head. She looked round, and when she saw Vyner she gave a sort of cry, and started back.

"Nora," said Vyner, advancing and holding out his hand, "I did not expect—I did not hope to see you here?"

What did the poor trembling woman answer? Nothing. She stood there opposite to Vyner, with a white and tear-stained face, and with

sad and startled eyes. The rain kept beating
down upon her, the rough dark waters of the
river rolled beneath the garden wall, the sky
was black with clouds. Involuntarily there
passed through Vyner's mind, as he looked at
her, a vision of sunshine, and the summer
flowers, and the smiles on a sweet, glad face.

The contrast touched him, pained him, fanned
the tenderness in the man's fast beating heart.

"And you came here," he said, still holding
her hand, "where—we were once so happy,
Nora?"

"I came," said Nora, trying to speak calmly,
"to—say good-bye to Roseland—I—am going
to sell it."

Somehow this idea was painful to Vyner.

"I am sorry," he said.

"Why should I keep it?" answered Nora,
with sudden bitterness. "It—it is nothing to
me now."

"No," said Vyner, and he turned away his
head.

"You might at least have come to say good-
bye," continued Nora, her face flushing and her
voice trembling. "You owed me this, I think.
You are right, of course—you are acting rightly,

but still—I—I—think you owed me this."

Then Vyner looked round.

"And why did I not come, Nora?" he said. "Because I dared not—because I had no right to come—because it is better that I should see you no more."

"Yet you came here?"

"Yes—to have one last look at Roseland."

"What is Roseland to you?" said Nora, passionately, and with a sob.

"You are unjust, Nora. What is Roseland to me? Shall I tell you?—but you know! you know!"

"Yet you never—"

"Went to your house? Nora, why should I go?—only to talk of things that could not be."

Nora was silent. But Vyner saw her eyes grow wet and big with tears.

"I did not go—" went on Vyner. "I thought perhaps you had forgotten me—it was better that you should forget me—but the other day I saw your face in the Park—and—and—the longing came over me, Nora—the old romance, folly, call it what you will; but I felt I must see Roseland once more—take one of your dead flowers away with me, Nora, as a memento of my own weakness."

A thrill, almost of joy, seemed to throb through Nora's heart as she heard these words.

"It was so bitter to me," she said, casting down her eyes; "so bitter that you should go away with a few cold words. If you had come—if we could have talked about it—"

"Well, Nora, we can do that now," said Vyner, and he smiled sadly, and once more took hold of Nora's hand.

Nora did not draw it away. She looked into his face and saw how aged and worn he looked. The handsome face was lined and sharpened, and Nora understood then how great had been the struggle in Vyner's heart.

"It is hard,—" she began, but she could not go on, for her tears choked her.

"Yes, said Vyner, " very, very hard—so hard, Nora, that I have felt sometimes I could not bear it."

"We must try," said Nora, softly, in her tear-broken voice—the man had touched the right string in the woman's heart. "We—we must help each other, Walter—for I know you are right."

"I have no choice."

"And—and—has it to be soon?" faltered Nora.

Vyner's resolution failed him. He could not stab this pale woman, standing before him with her tear-stained face, any more just now.

"I know nothing," he said ; and he coloured under his dark, pale skin, remembering at that moment his new furniture, his dados—all the things that he hated to think of !

"You will let me know ? " said, Nora, still in the same faltering voice, and turning away her head. " But come in now ; I think they have lit a fire in the house somewhere. We had better go in."

So Nora and Vyner went into the house out of the rain, and Vyner felt that he had been a coward. They stood together by the newly-lit fire in the drawing-room, and talked of things quite calmly. Not of Margaret, not of the old love, the old romance, but of pleasant passing things, such as we talk of, even if our hearts are heavy.

"I am going to drive back presently," said Nora. " Will you come with me, Walter ? "

For a moment he hesitated, but the temptation was too strong.

"If I am not in the way?" he said with a smile.

Nora only smiled in reply. Then she left him for a little while, and when she returned her face was no longer tear-stained. It was pale, composed, and sad, but the traces of the late storm were gone.

And all the way, as they drove together to town, no word was spoken of the old love or the recent sorrow. They talked as friends talk —friends, whose friendship has seen years; and though Nora's heart was very sad, there was no bitterness in it.

But just as they neared the house she said one word.—

"Walter!" and she turned her sweet face round, and looked into his, and held out her hand, "promise me one thing—whatever happens, let us be friends."

"If you wish it, yes—most faithfully, yes," answered Vyner emphatically, and he clasped Nora's hand tight in his firm and nervous clasp.

Nothing more was said after this of the days that were past or the days that were yet to come. But a promise had been made, and each felt that it would not be broken.

Then when they arrived at Nora's house she asked him to stay and dine with them, but Vyner said he could not, as he had not time to go to his rooms to change his dress.

"What matter is it?" said Nora. "There is no one at home but my father and the General and Lady Stainbrooke, and the General is confined to his room with one of his bad attacks of rheumatism, poor man!"

And Vyner did stay. Lady Stainbrooke, who was sitting, waiting impatiently in the drawing-room for her niece's return, as it was past the usual dinner hour, lifted her eyebrows, or what used to be her eyebrows, in surprise when Nora entered followed by the handsome painter. But she was too much a woman of the world to express this. She concluded, in fact, when she saw them enter together, that it was all settled; that their quarrel, or whatever it had been, was made up, and that her rich niece was going to make a fool of herself, and throw herself away.

Mr. Henry Sudely, Nora's father, too, remembered Vyner, and wondered secretly if his daughter were going to marry the painter. But as the evening passed on, Lady Stainbrooke

more than once put up her double gold eye-
glasses, and peering through them began to
doubt if her first surmise were right. The
flush of happy love was not on Nora's pale
face, nor the proud light in Vyner's eyes which
Lady Stainbrooke expected to see there, if a
woman with Nora's immense wealth had just
accepted him. They both were calm, pale and
composed; Vyner a bit grim in his manner to
Lady Stainbrooke herself, for he never could
forgive her, and Lady Stainbrooke—remembering the scene at Roseland—did not dare
even to mention Vyner's name to Nora after
he was gone.

Vyner walked home to his rooms in a very
restless and excited mood. The old love, always
deep down in his heart, seemed now so fresh
again. Nora's sweet face haunted him, her sad
wistful looks were pain, yet joy, to him. She
loved him, and he loved her so dearly, thought
Vyner—and, but for Margaret—

A letter from Margaret was lying on the
table to greet him as he entered his rooms.
Vyner looked at it, bit his lips, and a somewhat
strong and angry word rose on his tongue.

He lit a cigar and smoked it before he had

courage to open his love letter. Shall we glance
over his shoulder, and read it with him ?
Margaret wrote a most charming hand, and it
was very easy to decipher. The words were
very plain, and so was their meaning ; they
were exactly as follows :—

My dearest Walter,—I expected you to call last night, but
as you did not, I must write to you to tell you my good news.
Our house is quite ready at last. I saw the last set of
curtains put up yesterday, and everything looks lovely ; and
now, dearest Walter (as you told me to settle it), shall I fix
our wedding day ? I have thought of the 18th of the month,
if that will suit you ? There is no good, of course, in
deferring it any longer now. My dear father is very unsettled
and unhappy still about poor Nellie, but I fear this sad state
will continue until we hear something. from her, and I think
he would be happier if he knew that *one* of his dear children
at least was happy and settled. I shall make a point of seeing him every day after we are married, and our kind
neighbour, Mrs. Saunders, has promised to look after him
when we are away on our wedding tour. Thus my mind is
at ease about my dear father, and you must try to cheer him,
dearest Walter, about Nellie when you come.

I shall expect to see you to-morrow night, dearest. Tell
me then if the 18th will do. We might arrange to have it
perhaps on the 15th, but you must tell me to-morrow which
of these days will suit you best. And now for the present
good-bye.

Your affectionate and loving

MARGARET.

Vyner received this letter on the 8th of

September, and Margaret had fixed on the 18th for their wedding day! There are some things that are not good to look at, some words that are not good to hear. Let us then leave Vyner for a while after he had first read his love letter; leave him to fight out a dark, hard struggle with his rebellious heart.

.   .   .   .   .   .

He went the next night to visit Margaret. Up and down the room as he entered it, the blind father was walking with restless, uncertain steps.

He stopped as Vyner went in, and quickly held out his hand.

"Have you heard nothing, Vyner?" he said. "Nothing yet about my girl?"

Vyner was touched as he looked on the old man's eager, sightless face.

"No, Major Blythe," he said gently, "not yet. But we must have patience and hope."

"I try to have patience," answered the Major, "but it is very dreary, Vyner—to be always in the dark—not even to be able to look for Nellie."

"We do that for you," said Vyner. "You must cheer up, Major Blythe, and not give way; it is a great trial, but Nellie will come back to you yet."

"I am always waiting and listening. I dreamt last night the child came, Vyner; but it was very strange, I could not speak to her."

"You had the nightmare," said Vyner, trying to speak lightly.

"I tried in my dream to open my lips, but I could not move my tongue; I tried to lift up my hands to bless her, but they lay still by my side, and the child fell down and cried, Vyner, and I saw her face, and it was changed, and sad, and old—it was a terrible dream."

"They always go contrariwise, don't the old women say?" said Vyner. "So we must hope to see Nellie looking well and like herself."

"Yet I can't help thinking of my dream—I must have been dead, I think; if any life were left in me, I would have had strength to get up and welcome Nellie."

At this moment Margaret entered the room, looking very bright and handsome.

"Walter!" she said, advancing with out-stretched hand to Vyner, "that stupid Hatton only told me you were here a moment since.

Have you been here long? But you have been talking to my father."

"I have been telling Vyner my dream, Margaret," said the Major.

"And I hope he has scolded you. Walter, isn't it wrong, now, of dear father to indulge in such foolish fancies?"

"Unfortunately we cannot always help our fancies, Margaret," answered Vyner gravely.

"Oh, yes, we can. I never allow myself to think of things that I should not—I think it is weak to do so, Walter."

"Perhaps it is," said Walter.

"And now, dear father," continued Margaret, going up playfully to her father, and putting her arm through his, "will you go to your study for a little while, as I have a great secret to tell Walter."

The Major allowed himself to be led away quite meekly. Then Margaret went back to her betrothed. The secret that she had to tell him was to know whether the 15th or the 18th was to be their wedding-day.

CHAPTER XIX.

THE HOUSE IN THE GLEN.

On this same 9th of September—at the very time when Major Blythe was telling Vyner his dream about his lost Nellie, when Margaret was talking to Vyner of their wedding-day—away in the Western Highlands, by one of the most beautiful lochs in Scotland, a girl was standing in the moonlight.

She was quite alone. She had come down over the rough shingle at the head of the loch, and was now looking anxiously over the moonlit waters.

The girl stood there half-frightened, it was so wild, so lonely, and so beautiful, this silent glen. All around her the great jagged peaks towered up against the luminous sky, their shadows falling dark and weird on the valley below. No human creature but herself was to be seen, no sound but the mournful cadence of the loch breaking on the stony shore.

Yet the girl stood listening — she bent forward—what did she hear? The splash of the tide on the stones, or a startled wild duck on the wing? No; it was the measured dip of oars, and with a half cry of joy the girl recognised this, and in another moment or two, out of the shadow of hills, into the clear moonlight on the mid-channel of the loch, a boat glided into view.

Then the girl ran a few steps further along the rough shingle to the point to which the boat was apparently steering. She mounted on one of the big stones ; she stood there with the moonlight falling on her fair hair and her fair face. Two men were in the boat, and as the keel grated on the shingle a sturdy keeper leapt out and pulled the boat up on the shore. As he did this the other man too sprang out, and the girl stepped quickly down from her big stone and advanced with outstretched hands.

"Murray!" she said ; and Murray took her in his arms, and again and again kissed her sweet face.

"Nellie, what are you doing here?" he

said. "Child, you should not come out alone at night like this."

"I *could* not stay in. I was so anxious," she answered. "Do you know how late it is, Murray?"

"Couldn't help, my sweet one. The train got in late; and then with that confounded ferry to cross—and the row down the loch is a stiff one —it took us over an hour. Didn't it, Donald?"

Donald, the keeper, touched his cloth cap.

"A good hour and a half, sir," he said.

"There, you see, it is not my fault, Nellie. Come along now; Donald will look after the boat. Here, take my arm, and I'll help you over the stones." And he held out his arm.

Nellie put her hand fondly through it, and together, chatting and laughing, they commenced their rough walk up the glen.

Donald, the keeper, turned his honest, weather-beaten face round, and looked after the young couple disappearing in the moonlight.

"Aye, it's laughter now," he muttered, "wi' tears and moans to come." And with an ominous head-shake and a sigh, Donald once more seized his oars and began to make the boat secure for the night.

In the meanwhile the young couple were wending their way up the glen in the white moonlight.

"And have you been lonely?" he asked.

"Of course, I've been lonely," she answered, looking up smilingly into his face. "I've had nothing, nothing to do, Murray, but—"

"Well, what, Nellie?"

"Wait for you," she answered softly, and so they went on whispering the tale, old as the earth's first childen.

This young couple, now living in the lonely Glen of Strathearn, were called by their neighbours Captain and Mrs. Murray. That is, they had really no neighbours, but the house in Strathearn Glen was known to be inhabited at this time by a Captain and Mrs. Murray, to whom it had been lent for a season by its owner, Mr. Robert Campbell, commonly called Strathearn. But when some lady—one of his own relatives—asked Strathearn if his friends were people she could visit (the nearest neighbour being some sixteen miles from the Glen), Strathearn shrugged his broad shoulders.

"I do not think they would care to visit," he said; "and—I know nothing about the lady."

But Strathearn knew about the gentleman. He knew he was not Capt. Murray, but Murray, Viscount Seaforth, and he knew that he did not care that his relations should know Mrs. Murray. Thus Mrs. Murray, an innocent, fair-haired girl, had lived a month or two at Strathearn without being troubled by any visitors. The servants and keepers about the place made their own comments. Capt. Murray only came occasionally to the Glen, but the young wife lived there always. A whisper got about from a servant Capt. Murray once brought down with him from town, that the Captain had a right to bear another name than the simple one he chose to assume at Strathearn. Donald, the keeper, had heard this servant address his master as " My Lord," so Donald shook his head and sighed when the people about the place said how fond of each other the Captain and his young wife seemed. But Donald committed himself no further. What Strathearn had said to his relative, and Donald's head-shakes and sighs, were enough. The lonely house in the Glen was avoided. Strathearn's deer forest, lying beyond the Glen, marched with the deer forest of another proprietor, and the deer-stalkers on the hills used to smile and point out the white house standing in the valley below. A pretty woman lived there, it was said, and so the pretty woman's fair fame was smiled away.

This pretty woman had once been Nellie Blythe. Had Nellie seen the smiles and the shrugs of the deer-stalkers she would have smiled proudly back. She believed herself to be Lord Seaforth's wedded wife, and was content that for his sake the world should not know this. God did, she used to whisper to herself, growing almost solemn, as she often stood alone amid the wild beauty of the Glen of Strathearn.

But Nellie never suspected or dreamed that her good fame had been called in question. Lord Seaforth had told her, both before and after their marriage, that it would be utter ruin to him if their marriage were known. Nellie had faithfully promised to keep the secret. Seaforth told her also that they would bear the title for the present of Captain and Mrs. Murray. A friend of his, Campbell of Strathearn, would lend them a house, and Nellie naturally supposed that Lord Seaforth would make this one friend at least his

confidant. But she believed in and trusted
her husband with perfect faith. She loved him,
loved him most dearly, and she felt there was
no sin in her love. But she had one heartache
—a shadow falling athwart her love and happiness—and this heartache was the thought of
her dear, blind father.

More than once Nellie had broached this
subject to Lord Seaforth, but if Seaforth could
be stern he had been on these occasions.

"Nellie, would you ruin me?" he said. "If
the fellows in town once knew I was married
to you, I would have to leave the service, and
probably die in a foreign gaol. Wait, my little
girl—something will turn up some day—the
old man is quite well, I am certain. I saw
Vyner, the painter, the other day in the Park,
looking all right. Don't you fret. I'll find out,
if you like, if your father is well."

Nellie thanked him very tenderly for this
concession, and Seaforth did find out. He sent
his confidential servant, who had accompanied
Nellie down to Scotland on the night of her
flight from her father's house, to make private
inquiries about the Major.

This man, whose name was Clayton, picked

up in the neighbourhood some news of the Major, only part of which Seaforth reported to Nellie. He did not tell her—did not dare to tell her—all that Clayton had heard in the shops where the Blythes dealt, of the blind Major's restless grief and anxiety about his missing child. Nellie's disappearance had been greatly talked of. Her beauty, her youth, and the respectability of her position made this only natural. Then, poor Mrs. Saunders was never weary of wailing about her James's disappointment. James, indeed, had taken advantage of his disappointment, and made the most of it. He knew his mother would forgive him now when he came reeling home, and he therefore frequently did come in that condition.

He must have something to keep him up, he said, and the fond mother did not gainsay him. All his little peccadilloes were now put down to his disappointment, and Mrs. Saunders used to sigh and talk of Nellie constantly to all her acquaintances.

But the Major was not ill, Clayton told his master; and this Seaforth repeated to Nellie, with the slight alteration that her father was quite well. So Nellie tried to console herself;

but, sometimes in the moonlight; sometimes when the white mists in the twilight stole down the Glen, Nellie would see her father's anxious face.

If she might write him but one little line— she used often to think—but *one* to tell him she was well and happy, and that some day perhaps he would be proud of his little Nellie. But she was quite loyal to Seaforth. He was her husband—his wishes were her law—and so weeks crept into months, and Major Blythe knew nothing more of Nellie than he did the first day after she had disappeared from her home.

She led a very lonely life at Strathearn. Seaforth never stayed more than a week when he came to the Glen, and this was but his third visit there when we find Nellie standing in the moonlight by the head of the loch, waiting for his coming. But it would all be right some day, he told her; and so waiting for that welcome day Nellie tried to live on in peace.

It seemed all right the morning after his arrival, when the young couple went out together and stood looking at the sunlight flooding the vast gorges, the mighty peaks—

grey and storm-rent—by which they were surrounded.

The house in the Glen of Strathearn stood on a small natural table-land at the head of the loch, just above the rough shingle which the tide washed when it rose. All round the house, save on the side which faced the blue spreading waters of the loch, great peaked craggy mountains stood towering up, mountain upon mountain, crag upon crag. A wild, lone, and lovely spot, where mists and storms loved to dwell. But as Seaforth and Nellie went out on this bright morning the storms were still and the mists had vanished away. Each peak stood sharply out against the blue clear sky; the rifts, the patches of heather, the bare vast blocks of cold grey stone, all plainly visible.

"It always makes me think of solemn things —it is so grand, so still," said Nellie, in a low voice, and Seaforth smiled good-naturedly, and pushed some of Nellie's fair curly hair off her white brow.

"Romantic young woman!" he said.

She was leaning on his arm, dressed in one of her favourite white dresses, and her sweet face was all alight and glad with love. Seaforth

turned round and looked at her, and drew her
fondly to him. He had wooed her and won her
innocent heart for the sake of this sweet face,
and its beauty was still fresh and fair in his
eyes.

"Yes, Nellie," he said presently, with a half
sigh, "it's a fine place. If it were only mine,
child, we need not be hiding now."

"And is your friend, Mr. Campbell, rich?"
asked Nellie.

"Fairly so, I believe," answered Seaforth.
"The old Laird was a miserly old fellow, and
lived here most of his life, where, of course, he
could not spend much, and he quarrelled with
Strathearn—the present man—because he was
not quite a saint. I met Campbell in town
some years ago, and we rather chummed
together. He was kept close enough then, and
I helped him out of a hole more than once; so
when the old boy retired to the family vault,
two years ago, Strathearn, to show his gratitude,
asked me down here whenever I like to come.
He has a shooting lodge further up the hills,
and he always brings some fellows down for the
deer-stalking. I asked Donald, the keeper, if
they expect him at the lodge soon, and he

says they talk of him being here next week."

" But, Murray, does he not want to come to this house—his own house ?" asked Nellie, a little anxiously.

" He has lent it to you for the present," answered Seaforth, with a laugh. " Don't you worry, he won't come near you. The lodge suits him best, and he professes to be no admirer of ladies."

" I hope he won't come here," said Nellie.

" Not he. But Nellie, I promised Donald to go down the loch a mile or so and land, and try my chance with the blackcock. Will you bring lunch, and in the afternoon we can fish together in the loch awhile."

Nellie smilingly agreed to this plan. Seaforth and the keeper started on their shooting expedition, and Nellie remained idly about the place until she saw Donald rowing up the loch for the purpose of taking her and her luncheon basket down. Seaforth was standing waiting for her when the boat neared the shore, and he held out his arms to help her to land with a smile.

" Well, little wife," he said, " I hope you have brought something substantial to eat, for I am literally starving."

Donald, the keeper, heard him call Nellie "little wife," and the grim weather-beaten face and the kindly blue eyes of the Highlander relaxed into a smile as he did so. This Donald had groaned both in spirit and in reality many a time over what he supposed was Nellie's fate. In spite of all, however, her girlish beauty and sweetness had won his honest heart. He used to look at her sometimes with his solemn eyes, and wonder if she could be one of those against whom he had read such awful warnings in his well-worn Bible. Therefore, after Seaforth and Nellie had finished lunch, he said grace and ate his dinner this day by the loch with a cheerful heart. He even pointed out to Nellie with pious pride a lonely hut standing amid the wild gorges of the mountains, and told her how each month a missionary came over the hills and held a service there, and how the scattered shepherds gathered together to hear the word of God.

"And if the lady would like to go next Sabbath," suggested Donald, "that's the day we look for the minister."

Seaforth laughed aloud at this, but Nellie said softly—

"Yes, Donald, I would like to go."

Seaforth laughed again. He was a very careless young man this, and if it "amused" Nellie, as he called it, to go and listen to the Scotch minister, he cared no more than if she had gone to witness some heathenish rites.

"Only please don't ask him to the Glen, Nellie," he said, in his good-natured, laughing way. "I could not stand coming down some day and finding the minister's greasy hat hanging in the hall."

Donald groaned once more in spirit to hear these scoffing words. The minister's visits to him were as the "dew of the morning." They raised him above the crosses of his daily life ; they brought nearer the Beacon Light which burned so clearly for his pious soul on high.

"You must row me down to hear him, Donald," said Nellie gently, for she saw by the man's face how hurt he was by what Seaforth had said.

Donald touched his cap. The keeper's face was lined and grim and weather-beaten, but a sort of native nobleness of expression lit up this homely countenance. Born amid these wild hills, he had lived all his life face to face with their solemn grandeur. The distractions of busy towns, the rush of busy life, the stir, the struggle, had come not near him. No crowded *time* had made him forget or neglect eternity. In the stillness or the storm he heard the Almighty's voice, and hearing it, lived up to his simple faith.

His honesty and uprightness were well known. His father had been keeper to the Campbells of Strathearn before him, and now fifty years of age, Donald was not likely to change masters. He was a dead shot on the hills, and knew his duties well, and though the present Strathearn sometimes called him "that over-pious fellow, Donald," he both really liked and respected his old servant.

He lived at the house in the Glen, and had always charge of it in Strathearn's absence. He had made no fortune; for his hands were clean from "picking and stealing," as his tongue was from "evil speaking, lying, and slandering." By groans and head-shakings alone Donald expressed his doubts about his neighbours, and it must be admitted that this manner of denoting an evil opinion is safer than that of words.

Thus he had never committed himself by saying anything about Nellie, whatever his own private thoughts may have been. Strathearn had told him that a Captain and Mrs. Murray were coming to stay at the Glen, but Donald had noticed that none of Strathearn's own people—none of the Campbells—had come near to visit the lady. The women of the household, consisting of an old highland woman who acted as cook, and a young highland woman who acted as housemaid, had not been so reticent. They had asked Donald questions, but Donald had only groaned and shaken his head. He felt great inward satisfaction, therefore, when he remembered this as he sat rowing Seaforth and Nellie in the boat, after he had heard Seaforth call Nellie with his own ears, his "little wife."

The young couple spent the rest of the afternoon on the loch. Nellie would not fish. "It was too beautiful to do anything," she said ; and truly it was beautiful. On the broad, smooth breast of the water lay reflected, as if in a mighty mirror, the mountains and hills through which it flowed. There was scarcely a ripple on the tide, and above the sky was

deep blue and cloudless. Here and there a
wild duck skimmed, and a big seal raised its
head and looked curiously with its mild eyes at
the boat and its occupants.

"If the lady would sing he'd follow us,"
suggested Donald, as these creatures are popu-
larly supposed to be great lovers of music.
But Nellie only laughed in reply, and as the
big seal did not apparently find her laugh
musical enough, he soon vanished away.

CHAPTER XX.

STRATHEARN.

SEAFORTH only stayed three days longer in the Glen. His mother, he told Nellie, was visiting some of her own people in Suffolk, and he had promised to join her there. He told Nellie also that he had left directed envelopes in town with his servant Clayton, and that his letters from Scotland were actually placed in these envelopes before being forwarded, so anxious was he that no whisper of his visits to the Glen should reach his proud mother's ears.

But Seaforth did not tell Nellie that he still allowed his mother to scheme and hope for his marriage with "Crœsus's Widow;" he did not tell her that he also allowed his most pressing creditors to believe that this marriage was not only possible but probable. Yet such was actually the case. This, indeed, was one of

the many illustrations of how the miserable
influences of debt and impecuniosity will cor-
rupt and change the human heart.

When with Nellie amid the wild beauty of
the Glen, Seaforth tried to, and actually did
sometimes, forget his troubles. But money
embarrassments have a more faithful memory
than the tenderest friend. They will not be
forgotten. They follow a man wheresoever he
goes, tapping him on the shoulder alike in his
hours of merriment or woe. In the chamber
of death, how often the pale expectant heir
stands counting his debts! Even with Nellie's
soft hand clasped in his, Seaforth saw sometimes the grim shadow of the suspended sword.

But her sweetness and beauty always had a
good influence upon him. It was quite true
what he told her, that no contemptible thought
of their difference of rank made him keep their
marriage as a thing to be ashamed of, and
hidden away. It was not this, but the actual
knowledge that he was ruined; that his mother
would be dragged down by his ruin ; and that
he was really living on the credit of being a
young, titled, and unmarried man. More than
one of his sharp-eyed, beak-nosed, accommo-

dating acquaintances, had told the young lord, with a smile and a leer, that it was quite time for him to "*settle*." Many a rich City girl they knew would take him with his old title and his good-looking face. Then they heard the report about "Crœsus's Widow," and Seaforth had borrowed more money on the strength of it.

But on the morning that he left the Glen of Strathearn, as he parted with Nellie and looked into her fair trustful face, Seaforth told himself that he must do something—that he must change his plan of life somehow, and not bring any more trouble upon the loving woman who clung to him with such wistful fondness.

Nellie felt very sad after he left. She had gone down the loch with him in the boat, and as Donald rowed her up again he saw her blue eyes grow dim and moist, and a big tear or two roll down her smooth soft cheeks. Then she turned away her head and bent over the side of the boat, but Donald knew that "the lady's" heart was heavy within her, and he longed to speak, though he did not venture to do so, of a comfort which was beyond the influence of the fickle moods of men.

The next few days were very dreary ones at Strathearn. The weather changed, and the mists gathered on the mountain peaks, and the rain and the wind swept down the glen, and came dashing against the window panes, and the waters of the loch looked dark and angry.

Inside the house Nellie sat alone, and a nameless sadness oppressed her. She tried to think of the future—the bright future—when she would go home as Lord Seaforth's wife, and put her loving arms round the dear blind father's neck. This was the future, but the present was very sad.

Living alone in this wild place, with only three servants in the house, and Seaforth so far away! She could not even write to him openly, and to the house where he was staying in Suffolk. Her letters were to be sent to his club *always*, Seaforth had told her, and the post only came to Strathearn Glen twice a week.

Then the first post-day came after Seaforth had left, and there was no letter for Nellie! Nellie cried very bitterly at this. When she was so anxious, she thought it was very, very cruel of Murray to forget her. Murray had not forgotten her, but he was bothered and worried to death, and hardly knew what to write to the poor child alone in the Scottish glen.

So Nellie had nothing to do but to wander up and down in the silent house. The mist still lay on the hills, and the rain came sweeping down the gorges. It was very desolate—no letters, no newspapers—only anxious thoughts, and vague fears, sometimes for Seaforth, sometimes for the dear father at home.

Do men ever realise—living in action, living amid the excitement and competitions of life —how women fret and pine in seeming rest and security? The moth eats into the garment that is laid carefully away, and so anxiety and care wear most the hearts that are shut out from the struggle and stir of the world. But Seaforth never thought of this, or perhaps he would have contrived that his Nellie should receive one letter at least on the rare visits of the post-bag to the Glen of Strathearn.

At last the sun shone out again, and Nellie could get out and watch the mists and the clouds creeping, as if unwillingly, away over the mountains' peaks; she went out on the loch (glad of any change), and Donald rowed her down to where a famous fishing stream flowed into the loch. Donald moored the boat in a little bay, and then left Nellie sitting on some lichen-grown rocks, looking wistfully over the blue waters at her feet and to the blue misty mountains beyond.

Not a human soul was to be seen. Donald had disappeared up the stream with his fishing gear, and Nellie sat there amid the great stillness. But before long she heard some shots on the hills. She looked around, but no sportsmen were visible, and so she sat on, thinking of the past, and weaving hopes for the days that had not come.

But her day-dream was strangely broken.

"Donald! Donald!" she presently heard someone call through the clear air, and rising in surprise, she saw the next minute a tall man in a rough shooting dress coming hastily striding down the hilly ground behind her, and apparently making direct for the spot where she now stood.

He advanced straight towards her. Then, when a few steps apart, he slightly touched his cap.

"Excuse me addressing you," he said, "but

can you tell me where Donald, the keeper, is?"

"He is fishing up the stream," answered Nellie, in her fresh girlish voice.

"I want help very badly," continued the tall man. "The poor fellow out with me on the hills there, my keeper, has fallen down apparently in a fit, and is in a terrible state. I can make nothing of him, and I saw Donald moor the boat in the bay awhile since, and so if you can direct me to him—"

"Can I be of any use?" said Nellie, looking with her clear, frank eyes in the tall man's face, who on his part was regarding her with considerable surprise. "There is some fresh water in the boat, I think. Shall I run and get it? And if you will tell me where the poor keeper is—"

"You are very good," said the tall man, as Nellie paused. He was still looking wonderingly at the fair girlish face before him. "You are Mrs. Murray, are you not?" he added, somewhat abruptly. "The lady living in the Glen?"

"Yes," answered Nellie, her rosy colour deepening on her smooth cheek.

"I thought so—seeing you with Donald—I am Robert Campbell, of Strathearn."

Nellie had guessed this before. She had heard Seaforth describe their host at Strathearn as a "tremendous fellow, all loosely hung together," and looking at the brown, healthy, rather handsome face of the long-limbed giant before her, Nellie at once had decided that this must be Mr. Campbell, commonly called Strathearn.

"Shall we get the water?" said Nellie. "I am almost sure Donald has some in the boat?"

"Thanks. Let me help you over these rough stones!" answered Strathearn, and he held out one of his big hands. But Nellie needed no help. She sprang lightly over the jutting rocks, and soon reached the boat, and found Donald's stone water-bottle, from which he was wont to dilute his whisky.

"I have a flask with me, so we're all right," said Strathearn. "Here, let me carry the water. Do you know anything about fits? This fellow Brady, his face is so horribly twisted, perhaps it may frighten you to look at him?"

As Strathearn said this Nellie had jumped out of the boat with the stone water-bottle in her hand, and was evidently preparing to follow

Strathearn to the poor keeper who had taken the fit. But Strathearn, glancing at her youthful face, at her white dress, suddenly remembered that this butterfly—as he mentally was calling her—was hardly fit to look upon the terrible struggles of the stricken, perhaps dying, man.

"I am not afraid," said Nellie. "I will stay with him while you go and seek for Donald."

Again Strathearn said, "You are very good," and then went striding up the steep hills followed by Nellie, until they came to where the keeper Brady lay on the ground, with his face all drawn up and contorted at one side. He was stricken with paralysis, and had totally lost all power of motion over his body.

Nellie knelt down beside him, and bathed his brow. She took off her shawl, and made a pillow with it for his head, and she took one of his rough, hard, cramped hands in hers, and spoke kindly, gentle words.

"I will stay beside you," she said; "and this gentleman"—and she glanced up at Strathearn—"will go and look for Donald, and then we will carry you to the boat."

She did not know what to do; she had never

seen anyone in a fit before, but her kindly
womanly nature prompted her to act as she
did, and the big, tall man standing beside her
kept looking at her in the utmost astonishment.

"You're awfully kind," he said. In fact, he
did not know what to say. He was of rough,
though honest nature, and the women he had
known the most of had not raised his estimation
of womankind. He regarded them with a
sort of contemptuous good-nature, believing in
no noble qualities, but in a thousand frivolous
ones. He was no reader—the thoughts of
women who have writ their names in unfading
letters were unknown to him—he judged by
what he could understand, by what he had seen.

He was, therefore, quite astonished to see
a pretty woman like Nellie kneeling by a sick
man's side, her sweet girlish face so full of pity.

"Will you go and seek Donald?" she said,
addressing him a moment later. "The sooner
he is in bed and we get the doctor the better.
I am not afraid to be left."

"Very well," said Strathearn; and he turned
away. As he went jumping and plunging
down the rough ground over the hills, he was
thinking of Nellie.

"Artful little monkey, no doubt!" at last he decided, and his mind felt relieved at having come to this conclusion.

In the meanwhile Nellie was doing all that she could for the poor keeper. He had recovered consciousness by this time, but his articulation was painfully affected, and Nellie felt no small relief when presently she saw the figures of Strathearn and Donald hastening up the hill towards her.

This poor Brady, who had taken the fit, had been brought down by Strathearn from Warwickshire, where Strathearn had another property, but Brady and Donald had not pulled over well together since his arrival in Scotland. Donald regarded Brady as "a cross," a thorn in his side. Brady loved to speak in lofty terms of "what we do in Warwickshire." Brady was a sort of favourite of Strathearn's, and Donald (to admit the truth of so good a man) had been a bit jealous of the "English keeper." But when Donald saw the poor fellow lying before him, with his altered face and frightened, appealing eyes, all envy and bitterness died out of Donald's heart.

"It is a stroke," he said, solemnly, and knelt

down by Brady's other side, for Nellie was still kneeling on the ground holding the keeper's hand.

"If we lift him on the shawl, Donald," said Nellie, "you and Mr. Campbell could carry him more easily that way, could you not? And the shawl is a very strong one."

"If Strathearn will," answered Donald, looking at his master.

"Of course I will," said Strathearn. "But won't you be cold without your plaid?" he added, addressing Nellie.

"Oh no," she said. Her "shawl" was a pretty tartan plaid, and Nellie had wrapped it over her white dress when she went out. So the poor keeper was lifted on the plaid, and carried down to the boat by Strathearn and Donald; Nellie walking by his side, still holding his cold, cramped hand.

Then they lifted him into the boat, Strathearn supporting him in his arms while Donald rowed.

"May we impose upon your hospitality for a day or two?" said Strathearn, looking at Nellie. "It would be impossible, I fear, to get him to the lodge as he is now."

"I am sure it would," answered Nellie·
"How well it is that it is not far to the house
in the Glen."

Scarcely another word was said in the boat.
Donald rowed on with a swift sure stroke, and
soon the keel of the boat grated on the rough
shingle at the head of the loch. Then Strathearn and Donald carried Brady to the lonely
house in the Glen. The two women ran out,
and the dogs barked as they approached it.
But Strathearn was a somewhat stern master.

"Hold your confounded noise, and do something sensible," he said to the old highland
housekeeper, who was wringing her hands, and
openly lamenting over poor Brady. And the
effect of Strathearn's reproof was that the
poor man was shortly afterwards conveyed to
Donald's bed, and Donald despatched on a stout
pony in search of a doctor.

Nellie left the two women and Strathearn to
look after the keeper when they arrived at the
house. She felt she might be in the way,
so she took off her hat and went into the
rather scantily-furnished sitting-room which
was dignified with the name of drawing-room
at the house in the Glen.

This sitting-room had two windows, one looking down the loch, and the other on the steep mountain side, which stood immediately in front of it. Nellie sat down by this window, looking vaguely at the great storm-cleft crags before her. But presently a loud rap came on the sitting-room door. Nellie turned round, and as she did so Strathearn walked into the room.

" I am sorry about giving you all this trouble," he said, in his somewhat brusque way.

" It has been no trouble," answered Nellie. " I only hope the poor man will recover. Does he seem any better now ?"

" Don't know. He has a queer look, and I'm afraid it's a bad business for him. So you live here do you—all alone in the Glen ?"

As Strathearn said the last few words he was standing before Nellie, looking at her fixedly.

" I am very often alone," answered Nellie, and she looked up at Strathearn as she spoke.

She saw rather a good-looking face, with a distinct mark on his brow where the peak of his cap ended. This mark showed he had once been fair-skinned, but he was fair-skinned no

longer. He was a deep, ruddy, healthy brown,
with a thick brown moustache shading his
roughly-cut mouth, and thus decidedly improv-
ing his appearance, for his other features were
good. He had a good nose, bright, honest
grey eyes, and a fine square brow. And he
was almost a giant, long-limbed and careless of
bearing, and certainly not graceful in his move-
ments. Yet, taking him altogether, he was
good-looking—men, at least, considered him
good-looking, and women said Strathearn
would be handsome if he were not so *gauche*
and so shy.

" You had Seaforth down a while ago, had
you not ? " he continued, still looking steadily
on Nellie's fair face.

Nellie blushed ; she moved uneasily, then
she answered—

"Yes ; but you know, do you not, that Lord Seaforth does not wish his name mentioned here ? "

Strathearn nodded his head.

"I know," he said. "Awfully hard up, isn't he?"
Nellie blushed deeper still.

" I—I—don't know," she hesitated.

" Oh yes—horrid nuisance—know what it is,
for I once was hard up enough myself. But we

needn't talk about it. I was sorry to miss Seaforth—I beg his pardon, Captain Murray, when he was here." And Strathearn laughed.

" He—he spoke about you," said Nellie, and she cast down her eyes. She felt uncomfortable under the fixed gaze that Strathearn still kept upon her face.

" Is he coming back soon ? "

" I cannot tell—I am not quite sure."

" Humph—cool of him, rather, I must say, burying a pretty woman like you alive down here ! Have you books and papers sent to amuse you ? "

" There are some books lying about," she answered coldly, for she felt annoyed by Strathearn's manner.

" Humph !" again said Strathearn, and then he began walking up and down the drawing-room, with his long strides, and Nellie turned her head and looked out of the window.

" My father died here," he said presently. " Eccentric old fellow. He kept me horribly close. Seaforth was a good friend to me more than once in those days. You tell him when you write, if he wants a lift just now let him come to me. I've a few spare hundreds he's heartily welcome to."

Nellie felt dreadfully embarrassed. She did not know what to say, and kept earnestly hoping that this rough, big man would go away. But Strathearn seemed in no hurry. He kept walking up and down the room, looking all the while at the girlish form sitting by the window.

"It must be awfully dull for you here?" he said.

"It is very quiet," said Nellie.

"Should think so, indeed! But I must be off. You tell Seaforth what I said—I'll look in to-morrow to inquire about Brady. Good day." And Strathearn held out one of his big brown hands, and a few minutes later Nellie saw him disappear up the Glen on his way to the shooting lodge.

But before the day was over a great parcel of books, fastened together by a leather strap (a most miscellaneous collection) was brought to Nellie.

"Strathearn sent them down for the lady," said the messenger who brought them, and as Nellie undid the strap a feeling of uneasiness crept into her heart—she wished that she had not met Strathearn upon the hills.

CHAPTER XXI.

BORROWING.

THE next day the doctor arrived at Strathearn to see after the unfortunate keeper. He could not manage to get before, he said to Nellie, when she went out into the hall to speak to him, and to ask after the condition of poor Brady.

The doctor had a shrewd, brown face, and shrewd, brown, jocular eyes. He looked like a man who enjoyed many a private chuckle, but he was slow though sure of speech. He was pleased when Nellie went out to speak to him, for he had heard of the pretty woman living at the Glen, and was therefore glad of the opportunity of seeing her.

"I hope he will recover?" said Nellie, inquiringly.

"This time—partially," answered Dr. Macduff, his twinkling brown eyes fixed on Nellie's face.

"Do you think—" said Nellie.

"Doctor's shouldn't think, they should know, eh?" said the doctor facetiously, and he made a movement as if he wished to go into the sitting-room, and thus have a little further conversation with Nellie.

In common courtesy Nellie could not keep him standing at the door after this. So the doctor followed her into the room, and Nellie pointed to a chair.

"How do you like Strathearn?" inquired Dr. Macduff.

"It is very beautiful," said Nellie.

"Plenty of time for meditation, eh?" said the doctor, chuckling.

Nellie laughed.

"Bad place for doctors to live in about here," continued the doctor. "Air's too good for our profession."

"I am glad to hear that."

"Do you mean to make a long stay, then?" inquired Macduff, perhaps with faint hopes of a possible patient.

"I do not know," answered Nellie gravely.

"Strathearn should get a wife, and settle in the Glen," proceeded the doctor. "Ah—he's a wild lad you—the old laird and he could never hit it off."

"I have only seen him once."

"Humph! Some folks says the less the better," said the doctor, and having given Nellie this hint he took his leave.

After he was gone Nellie sat down to write to her Murray. She told him, we may be sure, all about the keeper's illness, how Strathearn had sent her down some books from the lodge, and she even added the doctor's "hint."

I hope he will not come here, dear Murray (she wrote) ; there is something in his manner that I do not quite like. At least I hope he will not come till you return. When is that bright day to be? Ah, Murray, Murray, if you were but always here—

Nellie was actually writing these words to Lord Seaforth, about Strathearn, when Strathearn himself once more appeared at the Glen.

Nellie heard his voice in the hall, so she turned the face of her letter on the blotting pad, but had scarcely time to do so when Strathearn rapped at the room door.

"I have come down to ask about Brady," he said, as if he were making a sort of apology for intruding on Nellie. "Good morning," and he held out one of his big hands. "So I hear you've had the doctor ? Did you see him? What did he say ?"

"Very little," answered Nellie, in reply to Strathearn's questions. "I fancy, though, that he thinks the poor keeper's very ill."

"Of course, he's very ill. It's a bore for you. We must get him to the lodge ; it would never do for him to join the majority, as folks say here."

"Do you mean—to die ?"

"Yes. That would frighten away some of the pink paint out of your cheeks, eh ?"

Nellie felt offended. She did not answer, and she cast down her eyes and looked very grave.

"Don't mean to be rude, you know," said Strathearn, noticing her manner. "I'm not a lady's man. I never can say the right thing to 'em."

Still Nellie did not speak.

"Did you get the books ? " continued Strathearn. "Ah, I see you did. Sorry I'd no better to send. I've ordered a fresh lot from Glasgow for you this morning."

" I am sorry," said Nellie, much annoyed.
" Oh, you should not have done that !"

" Why ? "

" Oh, I don't know. I would rather you
did not."

Strathearn laughed—rather a harsh laugh.

" Are you afraid that Seaforth," he said, " or
Murray, or whatever you call him, would not
like it ? "

Nellie looked up angrily.

" No," she said, " I am not afraid that Lord
Seaforth would be angry—but you are a
stranger to me."

Strathearn made a low bow.

" Thank you," he said, " for snub number
one."

" I do not mean to be rude," said Nellie,
" but—"

" All right ! You shall not have the books.
I'll make a bonfire of them."

Nellie's natural good nature now came to her
aid, and she could not help a little smile stealing over her pretty face.

" Why not read them," she said.

" Can't settle to books, somehow," candidly
confessed Strathearn. " It must be a great

help to a fellow who can, to get through the day. Are you one of the clever ones, then—you don't look like it?"

Nellie laughed heartily at this, for Strathearn was evidently so completely in earnest.

"I'm sorry I look so stupid," she said.

"Not stupid. But you're not one of those awful creatures who give lectures, and write books, and make a man feel like a fool! I've a dread, a holy horror of those women! By George! before I'd let any woman I had anything to do with stand up and give a lecture, I'd shoot her!"

"Then you must not marry a clever lady."

Strathearn made a wry face.

"I'm not likely to marry," he said.

"That is a pity, is it not, when you have such a pretty home?"

"Humph!" quoth Strathearn, staring hard at Nellie's sweet, innocent face. He could not understand her. He was not, as he had told her, a lady's man. He might have been, for his broad acres, his long purse, and his old name would have made him welcome in most drawing-rooms in Scotland. But he very seldom entered one. He lived chiefly among men and on the hills, for he was a devoted sportsman, and spent most of his time in pursuit of this favourite amusement.

Among his own people, the Campbells, he occasionally went into society, and there were fair maidens who would gladly have smiled on Strathearn, but he was too shy or too cynical to woo their smiles. He knew well enough many a pretty girl would have married him for the sake of his position, but he had never fallen in love.

"A fellow is afraid to be with girls," he used to say, in his rough way, " the old women pull one up so sharp." So he had kept out of the way of old women and young ones alike. He " didn't believe in 'em," he told his companions after dinner, and as he was now past thirty, he was just as likely as not to continue a bachelor all his life.

Nellie's fresh, fair face and innocent manner quite puzzled him. He saw, for he was no fool, that she did not wish to attract either his admiration or attention, and this seemed a wonderful thing to Strathearn, considering the circumstances.

"Did you live in London?" he asked, quite

suddenly, after staring at Nellie a moment or two·

"Yes," she answered, "in one of the small streets near Regent's Park."

"Humph!" again said Strathearn. "You are not very like a London girl," he added.

"I never went out into any society," said Nellie. "I lived at home just with my father and sister. My father was too poor for us to visit."

"Your father!" repeated Strathearn, in great surprise. "If you have a father, how did he, what did he say, about—Seaforth?"

Nellie's blue eyes grew dim at these words, and though she quickly turned away her head, Strathearn saw some heavy tears roll down her soft pink cheeks.

"Forgive me," he said hastily, "I am a brute—I did not mean what I said—indeed, indeed I did not!"

Nellie did not speak. She was really too agitated to speak, for Strathearn's words had brought back the ever reproachful memory of her father with great vividness.

"I am so sorry," continued Strathearn, beginning to walk down the room with his long strides. " I—I—do not know what to say—but I hope you will forgive me."

" Oh, yes ! " said Nellie, a little sob breaking her voice. " But—but, will you excuse me ?" And she rose and left the room, leaving poor Strathearn completely ashamed of himself.

He walked up and down the room, muttering that he was utterly disgusted with himself ; that he was " an ill-bred brute," for nearly half-an-hour after she had left ; and then, finding that she did not return, he strode out of the house, and away from the Glen, swearing that he never would go near it again as long as " one of those confounded women lived in it."

But, alas for human resolution ! Two days after this, one sunny morning, Nellie was sitting knitting by the left side of the loch, where she was startled by two handsome pointers coming running in a friendly manner towards her.

" Jack ! Jack ! Jean ! Jean !" cried the voice of Strathearn from behind ; and when Nellie looked round there was the long, lanky form of Strathearn following the dogs, and coming with his great strides down the hill.

He touched his cap when he got near her,.

and again called off the dogs, and stood there half nervously, evidently not knowing how Nellie would receive him. But this very morning Nellie had received instructions from Lord Seaforth to be "civil" to Strathearn if she saw him.

I hear Campbell is down at the lodge (wrote Seaforth), so if you chance to come across him, my Nellie, mind you do the civil to him, for after all it is good-natured of him to lend us the house. Tell him I hope to see him the next time I am down. I am awfully hard up at the present moment, and so can't come for a week or so. I wonder if Strathearn would open his purse-strings if I gave him a hint? Tell me when you write if you have seen him (and so on).

Seaforth had evidently not received Nellie's letter, detailing her interview with Strathearn on the hills, and the keeper's illness, when he wrote this. Nellie's letters were sent to him through his confidential servant, Clayton, and this of course always caused a little delay. But when Nellie saw Strathearn and his dogs appear, she knew it was Lord Seaforth's wish that she should be civil to his friend, and so she made him a little bow and gave him a little smile, as he stood nervously before her.

"How is Brady?" jerked out Strathearn,

though he was well aware of the keeper's condition, as Donald had instructions to go up with a report to the lodge every morning.

"He is a little better, I think," answered Nellie. "I saw him yesterday."

"I hear you are awfully good to him," continued Strathearn. "Donald—by-the-by, you have quite made a conquest of Donald—informed me this morning that the lady read more than an hour yesterday to Brady, some beautiful things out of a book." And Strathearn laughed.

"I thought it might make the time seem less long to him," said Nellie. "It must be a terrible thing for a man who was strong and well only yesterday to lie helpless there."

Strathearn made no answer. He stood looking down at this girl—this fair-haired girl, who seemed beautiful to him—and wondered, as he always did when he saw her, how she came to be in her present position.

"I—I—heard from Murray this morning," said Nellie presently, looking up, and with a momentary hesitation in her voice, as she mentioned Lord Seaforth's name. "He sent a message to you. He hopes he will see you when he comes, and he was sorry to miss you the last time."

"When is he coming?" asked Strathearn, and something in the tone in which he asked this question made Nellie once more look up in his face.

"I am not quite sure," she answered; "in a week or so, I think."

"Humph!" said Strathearn, in his rough way, and he jerked his large feet impatiently. "When he comes," he added, a moment later, "you will come out with us on the hills sometimes?"

"What, deer-stalking?" said Nellie, laughing. "No, I am sure I won't."

"No, no, not deer-stalking; but you might help to shoot the black-cocks."

"No, indeed! If I were to shoot anything— which I am sure I couldn't—it would make me unhappy all day afterwards."

"Lots of women shoot in Scotland."

"Then I'm afraid I won't be one of the 'lots,'" said Nellie, smiling.

"Well, I must say I don't exactly care for sporting women. A woman should be a woman, I think. I'd rather see a woman

—no, I won't say what I was going to say."

" Why won't you ? " asked Nellie.

" Because you might think I wanted to pay you compliments, or some such stuff. But I was going to say, I'd rather see a woman holding up a fellow's head, a fellow who was ill, as you did Brady's the other day, than I'd see her the best shot or the best fisherwoman in Scotland."

" It just depends on how you are brought up," answered Nellie, simply. " If I had been born among the hills very likely I should have been a sportswoman."

" Perhaps when you write to Seaforth—confound it ! I must get out of the way of calling him Seaforth here—when you write to Murray, then—you tell him the black-cocks are waiting for him ; and I tell you what, you must do the civil sometimes, and bring us out our lunch on the hills."

" Very well," laughed Nellie.

"May I sit down here?" continued Strathearn, throwing his lengthy form down on the rough turf, on which Nellie was sitting. "It's grand here, isn't it, watching the sunlight on the water ? "

. " It is quite beautiful."

"A nook out of the world, eh? Yes—but go where we will, bury ourselves where we will, young lady, worldly wishes, worldly passions cling to us. There was my father—he shut himself up down here, and swore he was done with the world and all things in it; but because I wouldn't go his way, be an anchorite or an ascetic, or whatever he called himself, just as he was, he absolutely hated me! That's no exaggeration; he'd have cut me off with a shilling if he could have done so, but the old acres were too tightly tied up. He couldn't take them with him into the family vault, but he would have done it if he could. So you see! He died in yon room." (And Strathearn pointed to the house in the Glen.) "Fancy him looking out on the loch and on the hills, with his heart full of hatred to his first-born!"

"It was very sad."

"I survived it," said Strathearn, with a grim laugh. "But do you see there—look down the loch, just past that clump of firs—and do you see a man on a pony?"

"Yes."

"That's the doctor—confound him. I declare he sees us. Yes, here he comes—he's rather a gossiping old party, I may as well tell you."

Strathearn was quite right. Dr. Macduff did see them, and presently rode up to where they were sitting, with an amused smile on his brown, hard face.

"Good morning," he said to Nellie, just touching his hat. "Good morning, Strathearn. Enjoying the view?"

"Exactly," answered Strathearn, jumping up. "We have been admiring you or your pony in the distance."

"Did 'distance lend enchantment to the view,' eh, Strathearn?" chuckled the doctor.

"Well, I think it did," retorted Strathearn coolly, staring somewhat superciliously at the doctor and his pony.

"How's Brady to-day?" asked the doctor, his brown eyes twinkling. "I hear you're very attentive, Strathearn, in your inquiries after the sufferer."

"Doubts, you see, about the efficiency of his medical attendant trouble me," answered Strathearn, with a rough laugh; and the doctor laughed also, and then waved his hand, and rode on in the direction of the house.

Strathearn looked after him.

"I had best go and see after him, I suppose," he said to Nellie. "Don't you forget my message to—I was just going to say Seaforth—to Murray, then, about the black-game. Good morning." And Strathearn touched his cap, and then walked away with his great strides towards the doctor.

END OF VOLUME FIRST.

TILLOTSON AND SON, STEAM PRINTERS, BOLTON.

www.ingramcontent.com/pod-product-compliance
Lightning Source LLC
Chambersburg PA
CBHW031040120726
47905CB00007B/2260